FALLING FOR THE CEO

S. N. CHRISTENSEN

CONTENTS

AUTHOR'S NOTES

This book can be read as a standalone in the fALLINg series and ends with a HEA.

If you plan on reading the first three in the series, I suggest you read those first to avoid spoilers about other characters.

Some content in this book may be triggering to some readers.

Trigger Warnings include mention of suicide, mention of rape, mention of kidnapping, violence, abuse, and the use of alcohol.

Chapter One

AMELIA

The beach. Everyone loves the beach. The nice cool breeze, the sun warming your skin, the calming sound of the waves, and shirtless hot guys walking around. This is definitely the vacation that I needed. I place my trashy romance novel down and close my eyes, enjoying the sun's rays on my skin. I can feel myself starting to tan, at least, I hope I'm tanning and not burning.

I lay in my beach chair and watch everyone that walks by me. There aren't that many people around, but there are plenty of unique characters here. I love to people watch and try to figure out their stories. One couple spreads out their beach towel, and the girl lies on her stomach. The guy rubs sunscreen all over her back and kisses down her neck. While I usually enjoy seeing a happy couple, now is not the time that I want to be watching this. The pit in my stomach grows, and I decide to move on.

A cute family with a little boy and an older girl is off to my left. The girl is helping, who I assume is her brother, build a sandcastle. He's looking up at her with a smile on his face as she helps. The dad grabs a bucket, bringing it to the ocean to get water while the mom is taking pictures. What a sweet little family.

Just as I'm about to start daydreaming about what my life could be, I hear my name being called in the distance. "Amelia!!"

I turn my head to find Sierra carrying four large bags on her shoulders, and she's basically dragging another. I sigh, roll my eyes, and get up to help her.

Once we get back to the spot I was sitting at, I ask, "Really? Why do you need all this stuff for an hour on the beach?"

It's getting late, and I know we'll be heading out for dinner soon. Sierra thrives on a schedule, especially her eating schedule.

"What? I barely brought anything! We have a full hour here. I'm going to need it all," she states seriously.

Sierra has a bad habit of over packing everywhere we go. Even if we're just going to the grocery store, she'll bring a giant purse filled with... well, I don't even know what it's filled with. Her purse typically feels like she carries bricks or weights. Being her, I wouldn't doubt if she literally had either of those things in there.

Sierra pulls things out of her bag and lays them out around her beach chair. She finally finds the sunscreen that she's been looking for and rubs it on her already perfectly tan skin. She has a darker complexion that makes her look like she always has a perfect tan. I don't think she has ever burned a day in her life, but she is always religious about putting sunscreen on.

She ties up her long, dark brown hair into a messy bun and leans back in her chair. She's one of the most beautiful friends that I have ever had, who is the complete opposite of me. Her effortlessly tan skin compared to my pale skin. Straight dark hair compared to my wavy red hair. Brown eyes compared to my blue eyes. She's tall and looks like a supermodel, while I'm average in height and average in looks. I try not to compare myself to my best friend, but it's hard not to.

"See anything interesting yet today?" she asks, also loving to people watch.

"No, not really. Just the typical stuff. There's not that many people here. It's a beautiful day and beach, so I thought it would be busier." I state a little bummed.

Most people like a beach that's not crowded, but I don't mind it.

"Well, you have to consider most people staying here were in meetings all day," she says, while putting her sunglasses on and leaning back into her chair.

That's true. More than half of this resort is rented out by her company. They do a yearly trip for their employees. It's a full week, Sunday to Sunday. We got in late last night, so we went straight to bed since she had to be up early this morning. She had meetings which lasted all day. Everyone is allowed a plus one, and she invited me this year since she currently doesn't have a boyfriend. She knew I needed the vacation and to get away. They only have three days of meetings, so we will have three full days to hang out together.

"So, I have some news..." she trails off, and I can tell she's trying to think of the best way to tell me whatever it is.

"Oh yeah? What is it?" I ask, studying her face for any clues.

She sits up and lifts her sunglasses to look at me. I have a feeling this is going to be interesting news. She has the face of she wants me to be open to whatever she's about to tell me. I know her well. We've been friends since high school. She's older than me, and I was a freshman when she was a senior. It seems odd to form a friendship like that and keep it going after high school, but we did. I've always acted much older than my age, and I like to think I'm pretty smart. I graduated from college with a 4.0 GPA.

"The company is getting bigger, fast. It's great, but that means a lot more work for me. They approved me to hire an assistant," she states, staring at me and not looking away as she watches my reaction.

"Oh, that's great news!" I'm happy for her because she's been under a lot of stress at work.

"Yeah, it'll help me a lot. I've been asking for an assistant for a while. Just someone to help keep things organized, run errands, set appointments, all that type of stuff," she says as she continues to stare at me.

"Wait, don't you already have an assistant?" I ask because I know she has Greta, who she loves.

"Well, I do, but Greta helps me with a lot of stuff. This would be more of a personal assistant helping with the minor stuff while she fries the bigger fish."

I can tell she's trying to keep her explanation simple. While I know she is high up in her company, I really have no idea what she or the company does.

"I'm glad they realized how much you do and know that you need help. Your boss sounds like a great guy," I state sincerely.

They really seem to take care of their employees and care about their wellbeing. She loves her job and says she couldn't imagine working anywhere else.

"It's a great company to work for and they pay well too..." she trails off.

Ah, there it is. I knew there was something. She's hinting at me asking to be her assistant, which I can't even imagine. Sure, we'd have fun, but I'd have no idea what I'm doing. I'd never be qualified to do the job.

"I know I'm going to get a teaching position soon. I've applied for a few the past couple of weeks and there's still plenty of time left for the summer. It's going to happen," I say and act like I'm positive I'm going to get a job.

In reality, I'm questioning every day if I'm going to get one and how I'm going to afford the bills. Most positions are already filled for the next school year, or if not, it isn't a school district that I care to work for.

"Yeah, I get that. You love teaching and you're great at it. What if you do it until you get hired as a teacher? Even if it's just for a little bit, wouldn't it be fun to work together?" she asks with hope in her eyes.

"Yeah, it would be fun, but I know nothing about your company. I'm not qualified to be your assistant. I don't have a degree in anything but teaching." I sigh, hoping she'll drop it.

We don't have much longer before we leave the beach for today, and I'd like to enjoy the last few minutes we have.

"You don't need a specific degree, and you don't need to know anything. You're smart, and I know you can answer calls, book my appointments, and run errands. I promise it'll be easy, and I won't be mad when you get a teaching job and leave. Please?" she begs, giving me her puppy dog eyes.

Usually that look only works for little kids, but somehow, she still pulls it off.

I sigh. "Fine. I'll think about it. How much does it pay?"

It can't be that much if I don't need any qualifications for the job, but really, it's better than being paid nothing. Like she said, I can quit when I get my teaching position, hopefully in a couple of months. I'm sure it pays better than being a sub in the school system.

"It starts at $70,000 a year," she says with a smile on her face.

I gasp and can't hide my shock. "Say what?! You did not just say seven with four zeros after it!"

"Yeah, I know it's not amazing pay, but it's pretty good," she says, knowing full well that's more than I would make as a teacher.

Like, that's almost double what I was making as a teacher in my old town. How can I say no to that? I do love teaching, so

I'll definitely continue applying, but that really does sound too good to be true.

"Okay, I guess I'll do it." I roll my eyes like I'm doing it as a favor to her.

We both laugh because we know that's not true.

"You also get full benefits, so vacation time and your health insurance will be paid for completely..." she trails off.

"Wait, they pay health insurance? Like I won't pay a premium?" I ask, again in shock.

"Yeah, they pay it all. You won't pay a penny for the premium. There are a lot of other benefits, too. I'll send over the packet information. I'll also send the application, but of course you already have the job because I'm the one hiring for it. We just need all your information for the system," she says, getting really excited.

"Okay, I'll fill that out when you send it. When do I start?"

I hope it's soon because I really do need the money. Sierra has a nice apartment that she's renting, and it's pretty big, with a couple of extra empty rooms. She's been letting me stay with her and hasn't asked for any rent money, but I want to be able to pay her. Plus, I'm running out of money and barely able to buy food.

"You can start in three weeks," she says with a smile.

"Great." I lay back in my chair, soaking in the last bit of sun for the day.

CHAPTER TWO

AMELIA

After bringing our bags back to the room, we decided to have dinner downstairs at the bar. While she has to attend meetings all day tomorrow, I have absolutely nothing to do. It's supposed to rain all morning, so I figure getting a little drunk might not be the worst thing tonight. I can sleep in all morning and relax before our massages tomorrow evening.

Sitting at the bar, we start off with a couple of margaritas with dinner. The company gave her a generous allowance for food on this trip, so she told me to take advantage of it, and I fully intend to. The past month has been hell. Not only did I lose my teaching job I loved, but I also left my fiancé. I put up with a lot from him, but last month made me realize I needed to leave and never look back.

Sierra convinced me to move all the way across the country to live with her and start a new life. I was so depressed and after losing everything that I didn't see how it could hurt. Moving away from everything I have ever known, I moved in with my best friend. She hasn't asked for any money, and I just became a leach. I don't know where I'd be today if it wasn't for her. Honestly, I would probably still be with Jayden, my ex-fiancé, if not dead. Just thinking about him makes me feel sick. I finish off my margarita and order another.

Usually, margaritas aren't my go-to drink to get drunk, but they sure do taste good. I actually don't get drunk very often, nor do I usually drink. I never felt safe enough to do that, but this week is a special week. I fully intend to take advantage and live my life to the fullest. That means getting drunk, enjoying the beach, getting massages, and spending quality time with my best friend.

"So, what would you say if I left with a hot guy tonight?" she asks, looking at me seriously versus in the joking tone she usually takes with these types of statements.

"Um, I'd need to see how hot he is first," I respond with a smirk.

"Well, if you look down the bar all the way to the left, the guy in the plaid shirt, then you will see." She nods toward him without pointing.

I look down to where she said and find the man in a plaid shirt. The guy has spikey blonde hair, blue eyes, and a handsome smile. He's not looking at us, he's just laughing with his group of friends. He's cute, but not my type. I honestly didn't think he was Sierra's type, either.

"He's cute. Do you know him?" I ask, trying to figure out if he works for her company or is just a random person here.

"Kind of. We met a couple of weeks ago at work. We did a project together, but didn't talk much. I'm starting to feel the effects of our drinks, and honestly, it's been a while since I've hooked up with someone. He's hot. I think I'm going to go for it," she says with a confidence I wish I had.

Sierra isn't the one-night stand type of girl, and I don't think she has slept with that many guys. I mean, she's slept with a lot more than I have since Jayden has been my one and only. Ugh, I need to stop thinking about him. I haven't had much of an opportunity to get over him and everything he did yet.

"Go for it, girl. Have some fun. We've got plenty of nights together, but I need all the details tomorrow," I say, patting her on the shoulder.

I don't mind being alone, especially in this beautiful resort.

Sierra gives me a hug and walks over to the group he's sitting with. I forgot to ask what his name is, which she should know since she worked with him. I watch as they chat for a few minutes, laugh, and then finally walk off together. Honestly, I can't believe she just went off with him so quickly. Thankfully, she works with him, so I don't feel like he's some creep at a bar that's going to kidnap or murder her. Thinking about that makes me shiver and want to head up to my room. Now that I don't have her with me and I've had too many drinks, I'm not sure staying here is the best idea.

Just when I'm about to get up, a man sits down next to me. He asks the bartender for some whiskey, which I can't understand how anyone could possibly drink. I glance over at him and immediately notice how smoking hot he is. Like, oh my God hot. Like model, actor, movie star hot. He's the definition of tall, dark, and handsome. A perfect light tan, like he laid out on the beach for just the right amount of time. Messy dark brown hair as if he just ran his hand through it. The barely there stubble of a beard trying to form. The beautiful hazel eyes that can see deep into your soul.

Quickly looking away, I down my margarita. This needs to be my last because I'm definitely feeling its effects. I keep stealing glances at him as he drinks his whiskey and types on his phone. I really should head back to the room like I was going to, but I can't bring myself to move.

He turns to face me and asks, "Did your friend leave you here all alone?"

Holy hell, this man seriously has the sexiest voice. What is he even doing here and why is he sitting next to me, talking to me? I feel my mouth hanging open. How embarrassing.

I quickly respond, "Yeah, I think she's done for the night."

Crap, why on earth did I just tell him that I'm now alone at the bar? If it was anyone else coming up and asking me that, I would've lied. But he's so hot. How can I lie or even think straight near him? How can I think straight when I'm quite a few margaritas in? I don't remember how many I've had at this point.

He holds out his hand for me to shake and says, "I'm Bash. What's your name?"

Bash, that's a sexy name. I wonder if it's short for something or if it's just Bash.

"I'm Amelia," I say while taking his hand and shaking it.

He grins and continues, "Are you here for work or pleasure?"

Since he's asking that, I wonder if he works for the same company as Sierra. If so, why hasn't she mentioned this gorgeous man before?!

"I'm here for pleasure. What about you?" Wow, that sounded wrong.

He has a devious grin on his face and says, "Same."

The way he says that makes my cheeks flush. I know they are turning bright red, so I look away. I go to take another sip of my new margarita, but it's already gone. When did I finish it? I need to leave.

"Would you like to get out of here?" he asks and now I'm questioning if I just said all that out loud.

"What do you have in mind?"

What am I thinking?! I don't go anywhere with strangers, especially men. He clearly wants one thing, all men do. I don't sleep with random guys. I don't sleep with anyone, period. I slept with one man, and that's all I'm going to do for a long time. I think.

"Ever go for a stroll on the beach at night?" He stands and holds his hand out for me to take.

That doesn't sound so bad. He didn't ask me to go up to his room or anything, just a walk on the beach. That sounds romantic. Which it would be, if it weren't with a stranger. He's not trying to get me in his bed, but he could still want to kidnap me.

I shake those thoughts out of my head. Seriously, what's the worst that could happen? My life is currently in shambles. How can a single walk on the beach with a super hot guy make it any worse? Actually, it can't. In fact, it'll make it much better. So what if he's trying to get me to sleep with him? What's a better way to get over my ex and forget about the past? There isn't.

I take his hand and stand up. We walk hand in hand out the door toward the beach. It's nighttime, so it's pretty dark except for a few lights on buildings along the beach. I take off my sandals and walk barefoot, feeling the cool sand between my toes. The full moon is shining bright, glistening off the ocean water. The sound of the waves is so calming as they crash into the shore. This really would be the perfect romantic night if I were with someone I loved. Ugh, what is wrong with me? Why can't I just enjoy the moment?

He leads me over to a secluded part of the beach where there's no one in sight. He sits down in the sand and helps me down beside him. Normally I don't enjoy sitting in the sand, but I barely register it with him next to me. We're there for a few moments, just enjoying each other's company and the beautiful night. He scoots closer to me and places his hand on mine. My heart races as my head grows foggier. I turn to look at him, which is a big mistake. I can't get over how hot he is, and what he's doing out here with me. He's staring down at me with desire in his eyes. He's not making a move though, which I should be grateful for because all of this is so wrong. I should've never left the bar with him. What was I thinking?

My heart pounds even harder as we stare into each other's eyes. Fuck it!

I pull myself onto my knees and smash my mouth against his. My kiss is hard and needy. I grab the back of his head to pull him in closer and pull on his hair. He guides me to lie back as he rolls on top of me. I move my other hand up his stomach to his chest, feeling his rock-hard abs. I let out a loud moan.

He moves his lips from my mouth and down my neck. One hand pulls at the top of my hair and the other slowly moves under my shirt to my stomach. He continues to kiss down my neck as his hand slides up toward my breast. Bringing his mouth back to mine, his kisses are just as needy. We continue like this for what feels like an eternity until reality hits.

His hand slides slowly down my stomach and just under the elastic of my shorts. I gasp as the heat continues to rise in my center, but I quickly move my hand on top of his to stop him. He places his hand back on my stomach and continues to kiss me. I enjoy the kiss for another moment but know this has to stop before I let it go any further. Oh, how I want it to go further, and the drinks in my system are telling me it's okay to go further. This gorgeous man on top of me wants me, but I know I'll regret this in the morning.

I reluctantly place my hand on his chest to push him away. Taking the hint, he stops immediately. He hovers just above me, staring into my eyes with such hunger. He wants me, bad. That look almost makes me give in, but I force myself to roll out from underneath him. I sigh and look over at him as he sits up and rubs his hand through his hair. God, that's hot.

"I'm sorry, I can't do this. I so want to, but I can't," I say, looking away.

Feeling guilty, I can't look at him. I feel bad for teasing him, but I also don't know how much longer I can control myself. My mind is barely saying don't do it, and my body is saying just fucking do it.

He doesn't say anything, but I feel him slowly move toward me. I look up as his face comes close to mine. My heart pounds again and my breathing is rapid. I don't know how to resist him. Please don't kiss me again.

He places his hand under my chin and gently strokes it with his thumb while looking directly into my eyes. In a low, controlled voice he says, "It's okay, we don't have to do anything. I had fun."

He gives me a gentle kiss on the lips and lies on his back, looking at the sky. You're kidding, right? This perfect, gorgeous man just got even more perfect? I close my eyes and take a deep breath. I lay on my back right beside him and stare at the stars with him. He places his hand over mine, and we don't say another word as I drift off to sleep.

Chapter Three

BASH

I stare at myself in the mirror as I straighten out my tie. I look exhausted, probably because I didn't sleep at all last night. I kept replaying my actions and beating myself up over it. I've had my fair share of one-night stands, but it's been a while. It's not something that I seek out like in my college days. When I saw the pretty little redhead sitting at the bar, I couldn't keep my eyes off her. I just went down for a drink or two, not to pick up some girl.

I noticed she was with Sierra, and they looked like friends. Once Sierra left her, I couldn't help myself. I had to talk and spend time with her. I don't know what it was about her, but she pulled me in. I didn't intend to take things as far as I did, but I couldn't help myself. I've never had an instant physical attraction to someone like that before.

She passed out beside me on the beach. It's been a while since I've wanted to spend time with and get to know a girl. We didn't do as much talking to get to know each other as I'd hoped. It was nice just being in her presence and again, I couldn't help myself when she kissed me. Regardless, I didn't notice how drunk she was until she passed out.

I carried her to Sierra's hotel room, figuring she was her plus one. I had my security guy, Wells, double check the information Sierra sent in for the vacation, and I was right. Which means they must be good friends. Just something else to beat myself up over.

I'm not one to take advantage of girls when they're drunk. She really didn't act like it, nor did I see her drinking that much. She mustn't drink often, or she drank a lot more before I got down there. Not only that, but I don't mess with people I work with. Not that she works at the company, but Sierra does, and we work too close together for me to be messing around with a good friend.

With all that said, I have a problem. I can't get her out of my mind, and I want nothing more than to get to know her. There are hundreds of women around. Why do I feel so drawn to her?

My phone rings, bringing me out of my trance. My little brother's name pops up on the caller ID.

"What's up, Jake?" I ask.

He doesn't call me often, which is why I always answer when he does.

"Hey bro. Not much, just wanted to see how vacation was going."

Yeah, that's definitely not why he's calling.

"Good, heading out to a meeting," I state, hoping he'll get to the point.

"You're on vacation. You should be having fun, not working."

I laugh. "It's a work vacation, Jake. I'm not you. I don't party and pick up girls all the time."

He's silent for a moment before saying, "I'm heading down to Georgia for a bit."

My heart sinks. I figured it would only be a matter of time before he went back down there. I was hoping he'd find a girlfriend by now or our father would've hired someone permanently to do what Jake does when he goes to Georgia.

"Jake..."

"Bro, it's cool. I'm just going down for a few weeks to visit and get a few things done for work," he cuts me off.

"Jake..."

"Bash!"

"Jake! Don't do anything stupid while you're there. She's not for you. You'll find someone..."

Jake interrupts again. "Dude, I didn't call you for a lecture. I'm over her. That's not why I called."

I sigh and try to keep my mouth shut as he continues, "Dad's been extra... Dad lately. Just wondering if he's said anything to you about why."

That piques my interest. "What do you mean?"

"He's been... You know... He's been on my case more and throwing out threats. Do you know if something's going on?"

"There's always something going on," I reply.

Jake laughs. "Yeah, you're right. I assume you don't know anything then. That's cool. Go enjoy your vacation and get laid. Ciao."

The phone disconnects, and I close my eyes, taking a deep breath. I always worry about my little brother, even if I don't show it. We've always gotten along great and rarely get into fights. He has my back while I have his, but he makes some poor decisions.

He parties too much, he sleeps around too much, and he loves a girl that he will never have. Everly's like a sister to me, but she broke his heart. In fact, she broke my best friend James' heart too. I know she didn't mean to, and I still love her like a little sister, but damn, I wish my brother would move on. I also wish she'd realize she and James belong together. It's obvious to everyone but her, and apparently Jake.

I shake my head and grab my wallet off the counter, shoving it in my pocket before exiting the hotel room. Trying to push away the conversation with Jake is impossible. I'm always worrying about him. I wonder what my father did now to make Jake question that something's going on.

My father has always been strict with us. He pushed us and honestly, we were never good enough for him. I couldn't take it anymore, so after college I took my own path and opened my own company. He wasn't pleased, but he made it clear he didn't want me to take over his company, anyway. He wanted Jake to take it over. I was honestly surprised at that, but who was I to argue when I wanted nothing to do with him and his company?

There's a lot of tension between my old man and me, but there isn't any bad blood. We still get together for holidays, and we occasionally work together when it benefits our companies. I'd say our relationship is more like a business arrangement than father and son, though. Jake must think that something is going on with the company if he called me, asking if I knew anything.

As I'm riding the elevator down, it stops on the fourth floor. I sigh and take a few steps back to ensure there's enough room for whoever to get on. When the elevator doors open, I can't help the smile that appears on my face as I see who's entering.

Amelia. The pretty little redhead's eyes meet mine and her mouth drops. She doesn't move an inch to enter the elevator, she just stands there. The door begins to close when I step forward and reach an arm out in front of it, so it opens again. I hold the button down to keep it open until she finally steps in.

She doesn't say anything as she averts her gaze from me and stares at her shoes, or should I say, slippers. She's wearing long pink pajama pants and a matching button up top. Her hair is a mess, and she doesn't have any makeup on. She doesn't need it. She's beautiful.

I debate for a moment whether or not to say anything. Should I be nice and let her believe she never met me and last night didn't happen? Or should I make her squirm? I laugh to myself. Who am I kidding? Of course, I'm not going to let this chance encounter slide past me.

"Did you sleep well last night?" I ask as the door finally slides closed.

She doesn't look up at me as she answers, "Great."

The elevator reaches the first floor before I can fire off another question. The doors open and she bolts off, pretending I'm not even here. I follow her to see where she's going. The fact she's still in her pajamas makes me think she's grabbing a coffee.

Sure enough, I follow behind her as we take a few turns, and she steps into the line for coffee. I stand close to her, and she looks straight ahead at the board like she's trying to decide what she wants. I have a feeling she already knows but wants to continue pretending I'm not here. Yeah, I'm not going to let that happen.

"So, what are your plans today? Looks like it's raining, so I'd assume it's not the beach," I say, trying to strike up a conversation.

She sighs and mumbles, "Staying in my room contemplating my life choices lately."

I can't help myself. I laugh. She's fucking adorable.

"I've had many days like that. Is there something recent you're contemplating?" I ask.

She shakes her head. "You can say that."

The line hasn't moved yet, so we have a little time. I grab her arm, spin her to face me, and tip her chin up so she has to look me in the eye.

"I hope it's not because of last night," I state.

Her cheeks turn red as she blushes. She tries to turn away, but I tighten my grip on her chin.

"Last night, this morning... Yeah..." she starts, but stops herself.

"I don't regret it, and I'm glad I ran into you this morning," I say, letting go of her.

She turns back around and doesn't say anything as she steps forward in line. I can't tell what she's thinking, but I don't think I should continue pushing it. She seems to want to be left alone, but I want to do anything but that. I'm about to say something, but the barista calls her forward. She orders, and I step up, handing my credit card to the lady.

Amelia steps to the side. "What are you..."

I interrupt. "I didn't get to buy you a drink last night, so I am this morning."

She looks uncomfortable. "Thank you."

I'm thankful she doesn't argue. We head over to the other side of the counter to wait for her coffee.

"You didn't order anything," she states.

"I already had coffee this morning," I reply.

She shakes her head. "Then why did you come this way and wait in line all that time?"

That's a good question. Why am I still here? I'm late for my meeting at this point, but I'm not caring at the moment. There's just something about her that is drawing me in. I want to get to know her. No, I need to get to know her.

"Have dinner with me tonight," I say.

Her name is called, and she steps forward to grab her coffee from the counter. She turns around and studies me for a moment.

"I have plans tonight with my friend," she says.

"What time does it end?" I ask.

"Around eight," she replies.

I smile. Good. She didn't outright reject me. She really has plans tonight, so she might be interested in seeing me again.

"Would you like to get a drink with me at the bar after your plans?" I ask.

My heart is racing, and my palms are sweaty. What the fuck? Am I a teenager again asking a girl out on a date for the first time?

"Okay," she says, while taking a sip of her coffee and walking away as I follow behind her.

She doesn't say anything as we walk toward the elevator. Pushing the button to get on, the doors immediately open. She steps in and turns to face me.

Before the doors close, I say, "See you tonight, Amelia."

CHAPTER FOUR
· · · ● · ● · ● · ● · ● · · ·

AMELIA

Seriously?! Did that really just happen? Please tell me I'm still dreaming. Tell me I did not walk out of my hotel room, in my pajamas, hungover, with no makeup on. Why would I do that? Who knows who you'll run into when you do things like that?!

Of course I ran into Bash. Of course! What was I thinking?! My head was pounding when I woke up, and I felt awful. I didn't have the energy to put on some real clothes, makeup, or even brush my hair. I just wanted a nice hot cup of coffee to start my day. I wanted to clear my head and forget about last night. Well, boy was I in for a surprise when I got on the elevator.

I groan and plop down on the couch in the common area of Sierra's hotel room. She never came back last night, so I guess she had a good time with whatever his name is. Actually, I don't remember coming back last night. The last thing I remember was falling asleep on the beach beside Bash. I do remember waking up at like four in the morning still fully clothed and nauseous. I changed into my pajamas and brushed my teeth quickly before plopping myself back into bed.

Then I thought it was a great idea going out in pajamas and running into Bash. Ugh. If that wasn't embarrassing enough, he followed me to get coffee and didn't even get himself anything! What was that about? Did he just want to torture me? Because I know I look like a hot mess, and he looked like a God. He was so handsome in his suit and tie. Damn gorgeous men.

I tried to ignore him and hoped he'd go away, but clearly, that didn't work. Why did he ask me on a date tonight to the bar? I teased him last night and shot him down. I don't even know what happened after that. I was fully planning on not going to that bar again because I figured he'd probably be there trying to find a girl that is actually willing to have a one-night stand with him. That girl isn't me. Or maybe it should be. Yeah, this is why I should've just stayed in the hotel room and drank the icky coffee from the hotel coffee machine.

I sit lazily on the couch, scrolling through my phone. When I realize that I just spent two whole hours scrolling through memes and reels, I decide it's time to get up to shower. I get angry at myself whenever I waste time like that, even though I'm trying to get over this hangover.

Entering the bathroom, I pull off my pajamas and throw them in the corner. I look at myself in the mirror and cringe. I can't believe how awful I look. It's been a long time since I've gotten drunk and hungover like this, but dang.

I absentmindedly go to unclasp my bracelet. When my hand meets skin instead of metal, I look down to find there's nothing there. My heart stops and my chest tightens. No. I look away and back again at my wrist, hopeful that it'll appear and be where it always is. It's not.

My heart races and I look frantically, picking up my pajamas, searching through them in hopes the bracelet came off when I took off my shirt. Nope. It's not there. I take a deep breath and let it out. It's okay. It has to be around here somewhere. I probably took it off last night without remembering.

I race to the bed I slept in last night and search the nightstand. It's not there either. I pull the stand away from the wall, just to make sure that it didn't fall. Ugh. I tear the sheets off the bed, look through the pillows, check under the bed, and scour the entire hotel room. It's. Not. Here.

I know I had it on last night while I was at the bar because I was playing with it. I always play with it when I'm nervous or in awkward situations. I don't remember coming back to the room last night, so I'm not sure if I had it coming in or not. Considering I haven't found it and tore this place apart, I'm going to assume that it fell off somewhere between the bar and the beach.

I look outside to see rain pouring down. Of course it is. I knew it was going to rain today, but I thought I would be staying in, not heading back onto the beach. There's no choice. I have to find it. Sierra is going to kill me if I lost it. I'm going to be sick if I lost it.

Considering I'm about to go out in the pouring rain, without an umbrella, I forgo the shower. I throw on my swimsuit and a coverup. If I'm going to get wet, I'd rather not ruin my normal clothes. Throwing my hair into a messy bun, I make my way to the entrance of the hotel. I stand looking out the front doors and sigh as I see the rain hasn't slowed at all. I take a deep breath, let it out, and head out into the pouring rain.

Three hours later, I still haven't found my bracelet. I plop myself down on the wet sand and bury my head between my knees. I've searched this entire beach. We didn't even walk that far yesterday, but I made sure to push through all the sand to ensure it didn't get buried. Short of getting a metal detector, I don't know what else to do.

My heart sinks just thinking about having to tell Sierra I lost the bracelet. It's special to her, and she gave it to me as a token of our friendship. I let out a groan as I fall to my back, staring at the sky. Do I just give up? What are the odds that I find it? It could be long gone in the middle of the ocean by now.

I close my eyes as the rain drops splatter on my face. The rain slowed down quite a bit since coming out here, but I'm still soaked.

I jump at a familiar voice. "What are you doing out here?"

Sitting up quickly, I try to dust some of the sand off that's sticking to my skin. "Uh, hi. Bash…"

He smiles at my inability to form a complete sentence. He holds out his hand and helps me up to my feet. I push my hair out of my face and try to pat it down, like it's going to make me look a little more presentable. Ugh. Why do I always look like a mess around this man? He's still so handsome in his suit while holding an umbrella, keeping him dry.

"Decide you couldn't miss a day on the beach even in the rain?" he asks, smirking.

"Sure, yeah. Something like that," I say, looking down at my feet.

"What's wrong?" he asks with concern in his eyes.

"I… I lost my bracelet last night. It was special. I haven't found it."

"You lost it out here?"

I nod. "I think so… I know I had it on at the bar last night, and I didn't have it on this morning. So, losing it out here on the beach is my best assumption, which stinks because I'll never find it."

"How long have you been out here?" he asks.

"A few hours…"

"Amelia… Have you eaten lunch?"

I shake my head. No. I haven't eaten anything at all today, unless coffee counts. As if my stomach has been waiting for someone to even mention food, it growls. How embarrassing. That wasn't even a quiet growl.

"Come on, let's get you something to eat," he says, holding out his hand.

Oddly, I take it and follow him. After my fiancé, I'm usually really wary about men, but for some reason, I trust him. I want to continue looking for my bracelet, but I am starving, and Sierra will be done with her meetings in about two hours. I should eat something and get ready before she's done.

"What are you doing out here?" I ask him.

He takes a moment before responding. "I noticed you sitting here alone and wanted to check on you."

He noticed me? I know I'm not that far away from the hotel, but I feel like it's far enough that he wouldn't have been able to see who was out here. Whatever, I'm in no position to question what he says right now.

He walks me to my hotel room, and we stop at the door while I dig out my keycard. I dig it out a little slower than I normally would because now I'm panicking. Do I invite him inside? I know Sierra isn't here. She's still in meetings. Should I tell him I'll meet him downstairs? What do I do?

I swipe the card and open the door. "Um... Do you want to come inside?"

Crap! I didn't even think this all the way through. Does that seem like I'm inviting him inside for sex? Is that what this will look like to him? Why do I suck at these things so badly?

"Sure," he says and follows me inside.

Alright, now what?

"Do you want me to order room service while you're getting ready or do you want to go down to the restaurant?" he asks, placing his hands in his pockets like this is just as awkward for him as well.

"Room service sounds nice. I'm kind of beat from all that searching," I say.

"Alright, any ideas what you want?"

"Honestly, anything is fine. I'm simple. Burger, chicken tenders, fries... anything a child would eat," I state, shrugging my shoulders.

He laughs. "Alright, kids' food. I can do that."

I make my way to my room to grab some clothes and then head to the bathroom, locking the door. After turning the shower on, I turn around to find myself in the mirror again. Wow, I can't believe I thought I looked like a mess this morning. I look awful now. I close my eyes and shake my head. There's nothing I can do about it now.

I make the shower quick, throw on some foundation, and tie my hair back. I don't want to waste time drying my hair when he's sitting out there waiting for me. I grab a cute little sundress that hits my curves perfectly. He looks amazing, so I feel like I need to as well.

When I walk back into the common area, I find him relaxed on the couch with his phone. He took off his suit jacket and tie. His top two buttons are also undone. I can't help but stare at how handsome and fit he is. So fit. Those muscles...

He looks up from his phone to find me staring at him, so I do what any normal person would do when caught staring... I smile and curtsy. What the heck did I just do? His grin widens as he sits forward on the couch. I know I'm blushing, and I silently groan. Did I really just give a curtsy? I shouldn't have worn this dress.

I shake it off and continue toward the couch. As I try to walk around the coffee table in the middle of the floor, my knee slams into the side of the table, and I internally curse. I falter a little, but quickly straighten and plant myself beside him. A little too close, but I didn't have much of a choice. I'm trying my best to not show the amount of pain that's going through my knee right now.

His grin turns into a cringe as he inspects me. "Are you okay?"

"I'm fine!" I say a little too loudly and with a smile.

I'm anything but fine. Holy crap, my knee hurts. I want to look at it, but I'm scared. It's definitely going to bruise. It takes everything in me not to rub my knee.

"Are you sure?" he asks, looking down at my knee.

Ugh, fine. I guess I have to look too.

As I move my hand to it and look down, I say, "Yeah, see, it's fine."

I rub it and want to scream. It's so red and has a little cut. Geez, why is that table so hard?

To get my mind off the throbbing pain, I ask, "So how was your day?"

He sits back before answering. "It was good. Filled with boring meetings."

"Oh yeah, meetings suck. I thought you were here for pleasure?" I ask because he definitely said at the bar last night that he was here for pleasure, and he didn't mention work.

He smirks again. "I was at the bar for pleasure. At this hotel for work."

"Oh," I say.

What do I say to that? He technically didn't lie to me in that case. Not going to lie, I'm a little uneasy about that, though. I don't like secrets or skirting around the truth. My ex is a big reason for that.

"What do you do for work?" he asks, changing the topic to me.

"I'm a teacher," I say.

That's not a lie. I was a teacher not that long ago, and I plan to be one again soon. Alright, I'm not much better than he is with skirting around the truth. He's a stranger, anyway. One that I invited into my hotel room. What is wrong with me?

"What do you teach?" he asks.

"High school English."

He looks surprised. "I wouldn't have thought you'd teach high school. Do you like it?"

I shrug. "I do. It can be challenging at times, but I love the subject and helping students."

There's a knock on the door, interrupting us. I'm about to get up to get it, but Bash gets there first. I take this opportunity to look back down at my knee to see a bruise already forming and a bump. Great. I also realize how high my dress rode up when I sat down. I didn't even pay attention, considering I was concentrating on the pain. Quickly pulling it down, I scoot myself further away on the couch. Again, why am I so awkward?

Chapter Five

BASH

I grab the bags of food that I ordered from room service. After tipping the man, I head back to the coffee table and start placing the food out. I look at Amelia as she watches me with wide eyes while I continue pulling food out of the bags.

"How much did you order?" she asks.

I give her a smile. "I just ordered a little of everything on the kids' menu. I figured you could have leftovers."

She shakes her head. "I'm pretty sure I'll be set for the rest of the week."

I laugh as I sit down and watch her grab the to go box of chicken tenders and fries. She takes a bite, and I just can't stop staring at her. She's gorgeous and hilarious. I know she's embarrassed about everything that happened earlier, but I think it's cute. She's awkward, clumsy, and everything opposite of the women I usually find surrounding me.

She holds out a fry to me. "Want one?"

I grab it from her and take a bite. "Thanks."

"Please eat something, so I'm not eating alone," she says shyly.

I'm really not hungry, but how can I deny her? I grab a few fries from the burger box and eat those. I have no idea what I'm doing here with her, but I just can't seem to stay away. I'm not into the one-night stands anymore, but I'm also not looking for a relationship either. There's just something about her, though, that draws me in.

"Do you have any siblings?" she asks.

That's random. "Yeah, I have a brother. What about you?"

She shakes her head. "No, it's just me."

She doesn't say anymore, and I take pity on her as I can see she's just trying to find anything to fill the awkward silence. Though, I don't find it awkward at all.

"Where do you live? Around here?" I ask.

"No. I'm currently living in New York."

My heart skips like an excited child on Christmas day. We live in the same state.

"Currently?" I ask.

"Yeah, I'm not sure how long I'm going to stay. I moved across the country and am living with my best friend," she says and acts as if that's embarrassing.

"I live in New York too," I say.

"Oh really? Which part?" she asks.

"Right in New York City."

"Me too," she says with a smile.

After going back and forth learning random pieces of infor-mation about each other, she finishes her food and places the leftovers in the mini fridge. While she's doing that, I look at the texts that came in from Wells. I texted him while she was in the shower, asking him to get a team together to search for her bracelet. He hasn't found it yet, so I shoot off a quick text giving more of a description of it that she just gave me a moment ago.

"My friend is going to be back in about an hour," she states as she stands by the couch.

I take this as my cue to head out. "Alright, I should probably get going anyway."

I watch her as I stand up and grab my suit jacket. I slowly shrug it on and can't help but grin as she watches my every move like she's enjoying the show. Her face shows everything she's thinking. I love that.

We made out last night on the beach, so a quick kiss wouldn't hurt, right? I slowly head toward her, and she doesn't back away. I lift my hand to her face and hold it as I lean in for a quick kiss goodbye. She moans as my lips touch her. Jesus. That makes me instantly hard.

I meant for this to be a quick kiss, but she grabs the back of my head and pulls herself into me tighter. Placing my arm around her waist, I decide to let her be the one to break the kiss, because damn, I don't want to.

My dick presses up against her and she notices because she fucking moans again. I lose control and step forward as she steps back. I push her against the wall without a centimeter between our bodies. I really don't want to push her like last night, but her hand begins unbuttoning my shirt. Shrugging off my jacket,

I let it fall to the floor as she continues unbuttoning. Once she's done, I let that fall too, joining my jacket. She pulls away panting, staring at me.

"We can stop here. I can get going," I state, groaning inwardly.

I can tell she's thinking for a moment before she crashes her mouth against mine again. She breaks the kiss a few seconds later and says, "No. Let's move to the bedroom."

"Are you sure?" I ask.

"Yes," she says, kissing me again while unbuckling my belt.

Well, if she's sure, I'm not hesitating anymore. I lift her up by the ass while she wraps her legs around my waist. I carry her into the room she went in earlier and lay her on the bed. Without breaking our kiss, we both crawl to the middle of it.

She finishes unbuttoning my pants, and I take them off, throwing them to the side. I'm left in nothing but my boxers and she's fully dressed. I need to remedy that.

I start at her ankle and kiss my way up her leg. When I reach the top of her thigh, I pull the dress up as she sits up and yank it off her. It joins my pants on the floor. I push her back down and admire her. She's wearing black lacy underwear and a matching bra. I groan and kiss my way up her stomach. Did she put this on, hoping that we'd end up here?

"Did you wear this for me?" I ask, hoping the answer is yes.

By the way she's blushing, I know it's true. "Maybe."

I smirk. "You're fucking gorgeous."

I unclasp her bra and find a nipple with my mouth. I cup her other breast, feeling how perfect they are in my hand. She moans loudly and bucks her hips like she's begging me to fuck her already.

The rest of our clothes come off, and I've kissed every inch of her perfect body. She's shy, and I can tell she doesn't like me looking at her, but I do it anyway.

"You're so hot, you know that right?" I say as I kiss up her neck again.

She groans. "No, I'm not."

I stop and look her in the eye. "Yes, you are. I don't say things I don't mean."

I can tell she's uncomfortable, so I just kiss her again. She lets me know she's ready by grabbing my dick in her hand. I hiss and feel like a teenager all over again. With a few more strokes, I'll be coming all over her.

I pull away and step off the bed to grab my pants. I pull my wallet out and then the condom I have stashed in there. Crawling back on top of her, I kiss her forehead.

"You sure you want to do this?" I ask.

"Yes," she says with a determined look in her eyes.

She doesn't have to tell me twice. I rip the condom open and roll it on. Positioning myself between her legs, I look in her eyes as I push inside. I'm all the way in when I place my forehead against hers, both our breathing erratic. I still for a moment so I don't come immediately. Fuck, it's been forever, and she's so tight.

I start fucking her as my phone rings. We both groan, but I ignore it and slam into her over and over again. It rings again right after it stops.

"Ignore it," I state breathlessly.

She laughs but then moans as I fuck her harder and position myself to go deeper. I try to hold back as long as I can and will her to come. Fuck, I should've worked her up more beforehand. I just wanted to be inside her so badly.

Just when I can't hold off any longer, she tightens around me and lets out a low scream with my name.

"Fuck," I hiss and finally let go, crashing down with her.

I kiss her a few more times before pulling out and getting up to toss the condom. When I return, she's already putting on her bra and underwear. I grab my boxers from the floor and drag them on. I'm not sure what she's wanting now, but I'm not just going to walk out of here like this.

Crossing the room to where she's standing, I grab the back of her head to make her look up at me. I kiss her and she kisses back. Good.

"That was amazing," I say because I can tell she needs reassurance.

"It was," she says, smiling back up at me.

"Now what?" I ask.

She steps back. "Sierra will be back any minute..."

I nod, and we finish gathering our clothes around the hotel room, putting them back on. Just when I finish the last button on my shirt, my phone rings again. I groan and look at the screen to see Wells calling.

"What?" I snap.

"Did I interrupt something?" he asks.

"What do you need?" I ask again, this time my tone a little lighter because I know he wouldn't call me so many times unless it was important.

"We have a problem back home. Someone hacked the system and got some vital information," he states too calmly for what he just told me.

"What information?"

"We're not sure of everything yet, but some high dollar accounts have been compromised."

"How?!" I yell into the phone and peek at Amelia.

Fuck, I'm scaring her. I take a deep breath and try to keep my cool. I need to end this conversation and get out of here before I ruin things between us.

"I think it's best if we head back to deal with this," he states.

He's right. I need to be at the office dealing with this, especially if it's going to affect our biggest clients. They are going to want to hear it from me and not from anyone else.

I sigh. "Alright, I'll be ready to go in the hour."

I hang up the phone and try to calm my anger. This is bad, really bad. "I have to get back to New York. Something's come up."

Her face drops. "Oh, okay."

I step in front of her and kiss her on the forehead. "I'm sorry. I…"

"No, I get it. I hope everything turns out okay," she says while literally pushing me toward the door.

I step back with her pushes until my back hits the wall by the door. She grabs the handle and opens it.

"Amelia, I…"

She interrupts again. "Seriously, you need to go. Sierra will be here any second. Goodbye Bash."

She pushes me so hard that I don't have a choice but to exit the room. Before I can say anything else, she slams the door in my face. What the fuck?

I rub my hand down my face and head toward the elevator. With everything going on back home, I don't have time to think about this. I was going to get her phone number, but she interrupted me. It's fine, I'll get it from Sierra later. I guess vacation is over.

CHAPTER SIX

AMELIA

Weeks go by quickly when you spend everyday trying to apply for teaching positions and reading to escape reality. Sierra and I had a great time on vacation, which we both really needed. I've spent everyday trying to forget about the man that rocked my world, left me, and never heard from again. I told her about my one-night stand, or I guess one-afternoon stand, but I didn't tell her much detail about it.

Today is my first day on the job. Sierra has thrown me to the wolves. She literally told me to sink or swim, so I'm trying to figure things out as I go.

"Take these to Mr. Hale's office for me," she states and walks off.

Alright... Sure, I'll do that for you. You're welcome.

I get out of my seat and find my way to his office, which she never told me where it was. The nameplate on the door says Mr. Hale on it, so this must be it. I peek in first as the blinds are open, so I can see directly in. It's a large office with a beautiful view of the city. I see a man sitting behind the desk with glasses on, looking down at his computer. I squint my eyes to get a closer look because he looks familiar. Too familiar. My heart skips a beat, and I gasp.

I quickly run back to Sierra's office and barge in without knocking. I must look like I've seen a ghost because she immediately stands and asks, "What's wrong?"

"I had sex with him!!!" That's the only thing I can get out.

My breathing is fast, like I just ran a mile. I can feel my heart racing and the nausea surfacing.

"Who?" she asks, rounding her desk to get closer to me.

"Who did you send me to give files to?!" I give her an annoyed look in between my heavy breathing.

"What do you mean? Like you knocked on his door and he just banged you in his office?!" Sierra's eyes grow wide.

"What? No! I can't go in there. I can't see him." I'm panicking. I've never had a panic attack before, but I think I'm about to have one.

"Okay, it's okay, come sit. Tell me what happened," Sierra says, using her calm voice and pulling a chair out in front of her desk for me.

I slowly make my way to the chair, sit down, and close my eyes. I take a couple of deep breaths before a full-on panic attack occurs, or worse, I throw up.

"When we were on vacation. He's the one I was telling you about that I met. I... Sierra, I can't go in there and face him. There's no way I can do this. Can you just bring him the files, please?" I give her my best pleading look and usually she does anything for me, so I'm hoping she does this.

"You know I would do anything for you, but I can't. You're going to have to eventually face him because it's your job. You're going to be seeing him almost every day," she says while sighing and sitting back down behind her desk.

"I can't! You don't understand..." I drift off and feel the nausea coming back.

"What do you plan to do? Quit?" she asks with a smile on her face.

Now that I'm actually looking at her face, I can tell she's amused by this! How can she find this amusing when that's exactly what I'm going to have to do? I'm going to be without a job, without any money, all because of a dumb mistake I made on vacation.

"There's no way I can walk into his office. Do you know how embarrassing this is?" I close my eyes again and hold the files up to hide my face.

"Look, Amelia... he probably doesn't even remember you. I bet you walk in there and he won't mention a thing because he most likely slept with multiple girls while on vacation anyway. I mean, look at him. He's gorgeous and has to be the type of guy that sleeps around. Even if he did recognize you, he's probably slept with half his staff, too. You have nothing to worry about," she says, and her smirk fades.

I can tell she's really trying to calm me down, but it's not helping. When she says he probably slept with half the staff and multiple people on vacation, I feel a pang in my chest. Is that true? Does he really sleep around? I'm an idiot. All you need to do is look at him and you know the answer.

Hang on. How does she know about him sleeping with half the staff?

"Sierra! Have you slept with him?" I ask with my eyes widening at the realization that she may have.

She immediately opens her mouth and gasps. "What? No! I mean..."

She looks down and doesn't continue. Oh my God, she did! She slept with him too. I can't believe this. I have mixed feelings about this.

"You did! Why didn't you tell me you slept with your boss?" I ask and feel hurt. Banging your boss is something that you tell your best friend.

She quickly looks back up at me. "No, really. I didn't sleep with him. But... it's not for the lack of trying and flirting. He's never been interested in me."

I'm a lot calmer now because I can tell that hurt her. I want to make her feel better even though I'm in the middle of my own crisis.

"Sierra, you know you're the hottest girl in this building. If he turned you down, it's not because of your looks or personality. He probably realized you're such a necessary component to the company that he can't risk losing you. I bet if he slept with other employees and broke it off, they would have to quit. He doesn't want that to happen to you," I say, trying to be convincing.

She looks at me with a smile. "Thanks Amelia."

There's silence for a moment and we both look up into each other's eyes, laughing. I don't know if it's more of a nervous laugh or this is a ridiculous laugh, but we can't stop.

After a few moments of catching our breath, I'm finally able to speak again. "Okay, I can't quit my job, so I'm going to have to face him. You're right, he won't even realize it's me. I can do this."

I stand up and walk toward the door confidently while my heart is beating out of my chest.

"You got this! Let me know how it goes," she says with a smile.

I slowly close the door and take a deep breath. I try not to think about what she said about him sleeping with half his employees and others while on vacation. The tightness in my chest comes back, and I don't know why. It was just a vacation fling, and I figured I'd never see him again. We didn't even exchange phone numbers. We were never supposed to meet again.

While I still have dreams about him, it's not like I really want him. In fact, he bolted right after we slept together. I was pretty bummed and pissed about it honestly. Like he got what he wanted and disappeared. Though, what we had was fun... hot... sexy... amazing... okay, I need to stop thinking about this. I can feel my cheeks flush, and I'm about to go into his office this time! I can't do this. I have to do this. But I can't do this. Ugh! I have to!

I push myself toward his office. I pick up the pace and keep telling myself to just do it. Just do it and get it over with. What's the worst that can happen?

I get the courage to knock and his annoyed voice sounds through the door. "Come in."

I don't say anything and slowly open the door. My heart is racing a mile a minute. The nausea is coming back, and I feel like I'm going to throw up right here in his office. How embarrassing would that be? Any more embarrassing than sleeping with him? Yeah, no, definitely more embarrassing.

I lower my head as I enter the room. I know I probably look ridiculous, but I can't look at him and maybe he won't recognize me. I make sure my hair is in front of my face as well, but the front of it is parted enough so I can see where I'm walking. The floor is super clean and has a beautiful marble-like tile look to it. His office is a lot fancier than Sierra's is. I slowly make my way in without looking up and place the files on his desk.

Swiftly turning my back to him to leave the room, I say in a lower than normal voice, "Sierra wanted me to bring these files to you."

I walk toward the door as quickly as I can without looking like I'm trying to run away from him, but I want to get out of here before he asks any questions. I fail.

"There should be one more file. I asked for three. Can you get the third from her and bring it back please?" he asks in his deep professional voice.

What?! No, she said two files. There were only two files. I'm going to kill her if she made this mistake.

Without looking back at him, I say, "Yes, sir."

I open the door to walk out with my heart racing at the encounter. I make sure I don't turn around to close the door, so he can't see my face. I succeeded this time, but I don't know how I can succeed in bringing the other file. How many more times can I do this? This is so awkward.

Before I close the door, I hear his tone change and him say in his sexy voice, "Thank you, Amelia..." dragging out my name.

Shit! Are you kidding me? He remembers me! How can he even tell that it's me? I can't do this, I can't!

I run back to Sierra's office and barge in again with my eyes wide. This is the second time I've barged in and been lucky that no one else was in here. I slam the door shut behind me and say, "Three files, Sierra?! Three!"

She looks at me confused. "What?"

"He said he asked for three files, and you only gave me two! He wants me to bring back the third file. By the way, he did remember me! I tried to hide my face, and he still noticed me and said my name!" I'm having a full-blown panic attack again.

Am I going to lose my job? You don't sleep with the boss. It's against the rules for so many companies for this reason. You just don't... Ugh.

"Calm down, it's fine. How and why did you try to hide your face?" she asks, smirking.

"Ugh, it was so awkward and I'm so dumb. It doesn't matter. Now I have to go back in there and face him again. Just give me the third file," I say, sighing with my hand out.

She looks over at her computer and scrolls down, looking at something. I can tell she's reading, probably looking for the email stating which file she forgot.

"No, it clearly states here two files. There's no third, see?" She turns her computer around and I stare at it, reading the two file names that he wanted. There's definitely only two, so why did he say he asked for three?

My heart skips a beat. Did he want to make me come back in? Was he torturing me? Why me? This is why I don't do these types of things. I don't sleep with random guys. Why did I do this to myself?

"Okay, great. Can you just email him back, telling him he was mistaken, and that I gave him all the files he asked for?" I ask, feeling relieved I won't have to go back in there.

"Amelia, really? You don't email the boss telling him he was mistaken. You do what he asks. I don't know what the third file is, so you're going to have to go back in there and ask him," she says as she looks back at her computer and starts typing something.

"Sierra, really? You can't just email him asking which file? Then I can grab it and slip it under his door. I don't even have to go in," I say, knowing how stupid it sounds.

She sighs and I can tell she's hiding a smile as she clearly finds this amusing. "No, I can't. This is what I hired you for, and it's your job. I love you, you're my best friend, but the faster you deal with this, the faster I can get back to my job and you doing yours. So, go."

I start to feel a bit angry, but I know she's right. This is my job. I would email him myself rather than walking in there, but since it's my first day, they haven't set up my email yet. I need to get the courage to just go in there and talk to him. We need to put all this behind us and never talk about it again. If she's right and he sleeps with so many people, then he will have no problem forgetting about it.

I leave her office again and head toward his door. I sigh as I take a deep breath and knock.

When I walk into his office, I find confidence to keep my head up high and look straight at him. He's typing something on his computer before looking up at me with that devilish smile that makes me melt. He looks more professional and intimidating here than when he was at the beach. His hair is slicked back without a single strand out of place, and he's wearing a full suit. He's so handsome, and I have to push down the feeling rising in my center. I can't be thinking about what we did on vacation together right now. I need to forget about it!

He continues to look me over as I see his eyes travel up and down my body. It's quick, but I notice it. He doesn't say anything, so I know it's on me to start the conversation.

"I'm sorry, Mr. Hale, but we can't seem to find the third file you asked for. If you can tell me which one you need, I'll run and grab it," I state as professionally as possible while holding eye contact.

"Never mind. I believe I have all the information I need with these two files. Thank you, Amelia," he states, while also never letting go of our eye contact. I can see the gleam in his eyes, but I can't tell what he's thinking.

Does this mean he realized that he only asked for two files? Is he doing this on purpose? He clearly remembers me, as he knows my name. Is he going to say anything about what happened on vacation? Should I bring it up? Ugh, now I feel stupid just standing here not saying anything. What do I even say to that? I thought I was going to be professional, get him the file, and just move on.

"Is there anything else you need?" he asks, breaking eye contact to glance at his computer and then back at me again.

Crap, I must look like an idiot just standing here. I have to say something, but do I bring it up to clear the air or should I just leave?

"Um, no, sorry, that's it. Please let us know if there's anything else we can help you with," I state and turn to walk toward the door to leave.

My heart is pounding because I got myself all worked up thinking about bringing up the vacation to put behind us, but decided against it because what if he doesn't remember me? Maybe Sierra told him my name already, and that's how he knows it. She's probably right, and he sleeps with so many girls. There's no way he actually remembers me.

"Thank you, Amelia," he states professionally again and goes back to working on his computer.

I let out a sigh of relief and walk out the door. Before I can close it, I hear him say, "I hope you found your bracelet."

Damn it! He does remember me! Slamming the door shut, I stand outside it with my eyes closed and head against the door. I want to bang my head on it, but that isn't going to help the situation. I need to clear my head and figure out what to do next. I go back to my desk outside of Sierra's office and sit staring at the ceiling for what feels like hours, trying to calm myself. What am I supposed to do now?

Sierra comes out of her office and stands in front of me with a smile. "So, did you find out what file he needed?"

She asks me this question, but she knows there wasn't a third file. We both knew there wasn't a third file.

"He said he has all the information he needs with just those two."

I know she wants to know every detail about how it went in there. She knows I can't stand leaving things unsaid, creating awkward situations in the future, but that's exactly what I did.

"And?" she continues to probe with that smirk on her face.

She's starting to annoy me. I get it, I really do, but she doesn't understand how bad this can be! I might lose my job! I mean, I planned to move on once I got a teaching position here, but honestly, I've been thinking about the possibility of staying. This job is a much better paying job. If it works out, then I can see myself staying here. I love teaching, but sometimes the pay just wins out.

"And nothing. I told him to let me know if he needed anything else and left," I say, leaving out the part about the bracelet because she still doesn't know that I lost it. I haven't found the right time to break the news to her, but I know eventually I'm going to have to. Just not today.

"So, you didn't talk about it at all? He didn't say anything? Did he look at you in a certain way? You have to give me something here," she states, getting excited.

She loves a good romance story, but I don't know what to tell her. This isn't one of her books. It was just a fun one-night stand as we escaped reality. Now we're back to reality and that's it. I hope that one fun afternoon doesn't cost me my job, but I'm pretty sure I'm okay as long as we both pretend it never happened.

"No, we didn't talk about it, and I don't think we should. It's best if we pretend it never happened," I state, knowing full well that he definitely wasn't pretending it didn't happen.

What was the point of that comment anyway? I know he didn't care about me losing my bracelet that badly. It's like he's trying to torture me by knowing that he remembers me. I need to just ignore it and move on. I need to.

CHAPTER SEVEN

BASH

Our reunion was better than I could've imagined. Amelia is the most awkward and shy woman that I've ever been with. It's fucking adorable. It was hard keeping a straight face when she walked into my office with her hair in front of her face. She must've noticed it was me before walking into the office. I rarely keep my blinds open throughout the day, but I knew today was her first day. I wanted to see what she'd do, knowing it was me in here.

After dealing with the shitshow that occurred while I was on vacation, I was going to text Sierra to get her friend's number, but she sent me an interesting email first. She had been asking for another assistant for a while and then, while on vacation, she said she had the perfect person. I approved it because she's damn good at her job and the company is growing rapidly. When I read her email, it included the resume and application of her choice, Amelia. I instantly approved it even before my guys did a background check. I couldn't pass up this opportunity.

So, I decided not to contact Amelia and wait until she started working here. There were many times I wanted to say screw the plan and call her, but I'm glad I didn't. What happened this morning on her first day here was perfect. I couldn't have imagined a better reunion. I haven't been able to get her out of my head.

Of course, I've questioned if I should pursue her or not, considering she's now an employee. I don't mess around with my employees, but we had our moment before she started working here. Plus, Sierra made it clear she probably wouldn't be here long as she's looking for a teaching position nearby.

A knock on my door brings me back to reality. "Come in."

My brother, Jake, walks in with a giant smile on his face. He looks like a younger version of myself, but with shaggier hair. I'm a little bulkier as well, but we could pass as twins if we wanted to. He sits in the chair on the other side of my desk.

"What's up?" I ask him. I didn't even know he was back.

"Just wanted to say hi to my big bro," he says, keeping that grin on his face.

I lean back in my chair. "Okay... When did you get back in town?"

"This morning. I have some news..." he trails off.

I cock my eyebrow at him. He likes the dramatics, but I don't have time for his games. I love him, but I'm busy.

"Then tell me the news," I say, folding my hands on the desk, waiting.

"Someone might be moving back to town..."

My heart rate picks up at what he's suggesting. If it's who I think it is, then I have mixed feelings about this.

"Who?" I ask, not wanting to play into his game.

"Everly."

"Why?" I ask.

He cocks his eyebrow at me this time. "Because she's having trouble finding a job and our old high school offered her one here."

I sit back and laugh. Having trouble finding a job? There's no way she's having trouble finding a job. With her degree and GPA, anyone would be happy to have her. No, there's only one reason she's having trouble finding a job, and it's not because of her.

"She's going to take it?" I ask.

He shrugs his shoulders. "Yeah, I think so. She didn't seem too happy about it, but I think I've convinced her."

I shake my head. "Well, it'll be nice having her back... but Jake..."

His smile fades as he holds out his hand to stop me. "Bro, I already told you that I'm over it. It'll just be nice having her back, you know?"

I sigh. "Yeah, I know."

I stare at him, wondering if he's talking to James yet or if he plans to. I want to voice the question, but I know he knows exactly what I'm thinking.

"No, and I don't plan on it. He'll have to come to me," he says.

I shake my head. "I think you should extend the olive branch to him before she gets here."

He groans and stands. "Nah, I've already tried, and he didn't want to hear it. I don't really care."

That's a lie. Jake may act like he's carefree and doesn't care about what others think, but he's the most sensitive of all of us. Regardless, I don't have time for their drama. I love both of them. Jake's my real brother and James is my best friend who grew up like my brother. They've put me in a shitty position because I understand both of their sides. This feud they have and not talking to each other for years sucks. And it's all because of a girl.

Jake walks toward the door. "Anyway, I just wanted to share the news and let you know I'm back in town."

"Thanks for letting me know. Let's get some drinks one night," I say, meaning it.

We try to get together at least once a week when we're both in town. There are a lot of times he's gone for an extended period of time with work or just for fun, but when we're both around, there's no excuse not to. We've always been close, and I don't plan on that ever changing.

"Ben and I are meeting up Friday night if you want to join," he says while opening the door.

Ben is James' younger brother, who is also Jake's best friend. I'm thankful the fallout between Jake and James didn't ruin their relationship too.

"Yeah, sounds good. Just tell me when and where."

I watch him walk out and let out the deep breath I just drew in. I rub my hands through my hair. My brother stresses me out. I worry too much about him.

Just when I'm getting back into my work, another knock comes on the door.

"Come in," I groan.

Sierra walks in and stands behind the chair that Jake just occupied.

"How can I help you?" I ask her politely, even though I know exactly why she's here. I can see it in her smile.

"I'm heading out early for my appointment. I just wanted to let you know that if you need anything, Amelia is here. You have met her, right?" she asks, and I know she knows.

I nod and don't give her any tell. "Yeah, I met her. Thanks. I hope your appointment goes well."

I continue typing on my computer as if she's already left the room. Unfortunately, she hasn't.

"Is there something else I can do for you?" I ask, glancing back up at her.

Her grin widens. "Did you meet Amelia on vacation?"

Why does she always need to be so nosy? I'm the one who's done this. I'm too nice.

"I did," I state, not elaborating.

"I see..." she says.

"If there isn't anything else, then I really need to send out this email." I glare at her, hinting it's time for her to leave.

She sighs and walks toward the door. Surprisingly, she leaves and closes it without another word. I shake my head. This is why I don't mess around with employees. It creates too much drama in the workplace, and I have enough of that at home. I don't need that at work... but Amelia makes me want to break that rule.

I continue typing out the email that I've been trying to write out since Jake interrupted me, but now my phone buzzes with a text. Jesus, what now?

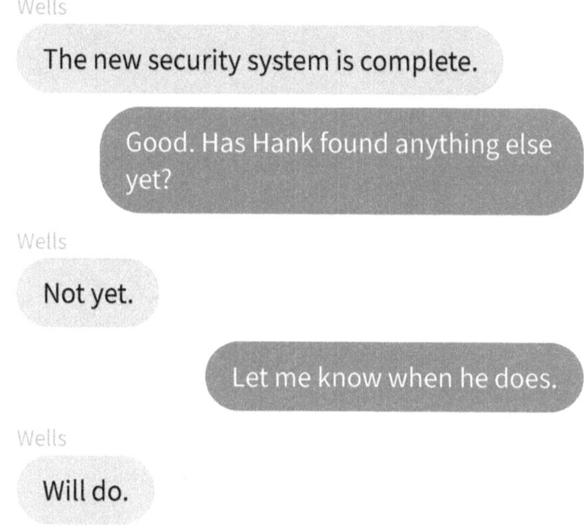

We added some extra security measures and changed our entire system after someone hacked into it, compromising accounts. Thankfully, they weren't able to get any information to do damage, but they could have. We're trying to figure out who it was and why, so we use a guy named Hank who is exceptional at finding information. I've never met the guy in person, none of us have. He's a hacker, and he likes to stay anonymous, but for the money, he'll help us with what we need.

I finally get back to the email when there's another knock on my door. I answer, annoyed, "What?"

My annoyance quickly fades when Amelia barely walks in the room with her head down and shoulders slouched. Fuck, I didn't mean to snap at her.

"I'm sorry to interrupt sir, but Sierra told me to remind you of your dinner meeting tonight at seven... I would have emailed you the reminder, but they haven't set up my email yet," she says it all so low I barely hear her.

With a soothing voice, I say, "Thank you for the reminder. I'll also make sure they set up your email before you leave today."

"Thank you, sir." She nods and leaves my office.

Fuck. Why is it that every time she's around, something is happening to make me annoyed? I feel like she keeps seeing the worst parts of me. I have to say, I do like how her presence instantly makes me feel better.

CHAPTER EIGHT

AMELIA

I throw myself on the couch in Sierra's apartment and groan as I curl up in a ball. I thought teaching was draining, but this job has taken every ounce of energy that I have. It's finally Friday, and I plan to lie here all weekend and do nothing.

After the first day of work, I barely saw Mr. Hale. He insists I call him Bash, but since he's my boss, I need to keep that line in place and that means that I call him Mr. Hale. He seemed to be in a mood every time I saw him on Monday. While I know his job is stressful, that's a big red flag to me. I cannot get into another toxic relationship after just getting out of one. I need to concentrate on myself. There are so many reasons I need to stay as far away from him as possible.

As I lay staring at the ceiling, memories of my ex, Jayden, surface.

After a long day of classes and exams, I finally walk through the door of our apartment. I set the Chinese takeout down on the little dining room table and head into Jay's gaming room. I peek my head in to find him playing some sort of shooter game on his computer.

"Hey babe, I brought your favorite Chinese home," I say quietly, but loud enough for him to hear.

He doesn't take his eyes away from his screen as he says, annoyed, "I'll be out in a minute."

It's late and I'm starving, so I pull out the food and start plating it for him and myself. By the time I'm done, he's still not out here, so I head to the bedroom to get changed into some comfortable clothing and hit the bathroom. Once I return, the table is still empty, except for our full plates of food.

I decide to go ahead and eat. While waiting for him, I read my book to forget the world for just a little while. College is a lot harder than I thought it would be, and working on top of my classes is exhausting. A good book always does the job of making me feel better.

I finish my food and wash the plate before Jay even makes it out of his room. Peeking my head in again, I find him still playing. I'm annoyed, but I won't let it show.

"Hey babe, did you want me to bring your food in here?" I ask.

This time, he turns around in his chair to face me. "Did you already eat?"

"Yeah, I was starving," I say.

He rolls his eyes. "Of course you were. You couldn't even wait a few minutes for me? Yeah, whatever. Just bring it in here."

I want to say something back, but it's not worth it. I run back to the kitchen, grab his plate, and place it on the desk in front of him.

He scoffs. "When are you going to make us a good meal?"

Huh? "I've had exams all week, so I haven't been able to make a meal. Hopefully after exams I can start cooking again."

"You always have an excuse on why you're so lazy," he says.

Alright, no. Did he seriously just call me lazy?

"I picked up your favorite food while I hate Chinese. I work thirty hours a week and attend college full time while you sit here and play games all night," I spit back and instantly regret it.

He stands up angrily, getting in my face. "Excuse me? I work my ass off everyday so I can pay for this apartment and save money for our future. My job is stressful, so I deserve to unwind at night with games. Are you trying to call me lazy?"

My heart races and my eyes widen. "No... I'm sorry, I didn't mean it like that."

His face relaxes a little as he cups my cheek. I flinch, not knowing what he's about to do. He kisses my forehead.

"I know, babe. I'm just stressed at work is all. I love you and just really need your support," he says calmly.

I nod but don't say anything back. I'm still angry at what he just said, but I can't set him off. Walking out of the room, I head to the bathroom, lock the door, and take a long shower to wash the day away.

The sound of the door unlocking and opening brings me back to reality. I sit up as I try to even my breathing. I still get so worked up thinking about Jayden and can't believe I stayed with him for so many years and even agreed to marry him. Why didn't I see how wrong our relationship was? Somehow, I really thought that he loved me and that's just how relationships were. I'm really trying to be kind to myself again and hopefully one day I will find a man who loves and respects me.

"Giving up already?" Sierra asks as she throws her keys on the island and slips off her shoes.

I laugh weakly. "I'm freaking exhausted."

She grins. "It'll get easier. The first week is the hardest because you're trying to figure out where things are and what to do."

She's right. It took me forever to figure out where everything was and what each floor of the building was for. Every time I sat down and during all my breaks, I studied everything so I could learn it. I don't like being caught off guard and not knowing things.

"I think the end of your first week calls for some celebrating," she says, keeping that grin on her face.

I groan. "Unless you're talking about getting on pajamas and watching Netflix with some wine, then count me out."

She grabs my arms and pulls me to my feet. "Uh no. You're coming out with me tonight. We're going to a bar, getting drunk, and seeing what hot guys we can pick up."

I laugh. "I take it you and work boy went your separate ways?"

I still have no idea what his name was that she left with from the bar on vacation. She didn't go out with him again, or at least, I don't know that she did.

This time, she groans. "No, we're not going to talk about him."

I shrug my shoulders. "I really don't feel like going out, Sierra."

"Pleassseeee," she whines with her puppy dog eyes.

I roll my eyes and groan. "Fine! One hour!"

She squeals, jumps up and down, and claps. "Alright, go get on one of your sexy little dresses. We're going to have a fun girls' night!"

I want to be annoyed, but I can't. Her excitement is contagious. I just shake my head and smile as I walk to my room to find something cute to wear tonight.

How is it that one hour always turns into two and counting when I go out with Sierra? We hit her favorite bar in the city and spent the first hour and a half talking and drinking. The next half hour was spent dancing. Now I'm sitting at the bar alone at hour two because she wants to dance with some stranger. I'll admit, he's cute. I don't know what's gotten into Sierra, but she's acting like she needs to find a boyfriend, stat. She's been single for so long and wasn't really looking at guys, and she definitely didn't go home with them. I hope she's not going to do that tonight.

My heart stops when someone plops into the seat beside me, and I stare into familiar hazel eyes. I take a few seconds to compose myself as I realize that it's not Bash. I look the man over to also find the familiar dark messy hair and same jawline. Holy crap, he really looks just like Bash, except his hair is a little longer and he's a tad leaner.

His smile grows as he realizes I'm checking him out. I blush because I'm not really checking him out. I'm just in awe that he looks just like Bash. Apparently, doppelgangers are real, and I just found his.

"Hello," the stranger next to me says.

"Hi," I smile back as I continue staring at him. I can't stop.

"I'm Jake," he holds out his hand for me to shake.

I take it and say, "Amelia."

"You here alone?" he asks, and I'm immediately on guard.

I haven't had as much to drink this time as I did when I met Bash. It would be stupid to tell a stranger that you're here alone. Thankfully, I'm not.

"Nah, I'm just taking a quick break from dancing with my friends," I say.

I use the plural term of friend because saying I have multiple people that I'm here with is better than one. That should deter anyone from trying to drug or kidnap me. Yeah, I've become a paranoid freaking person. That's why I was so concerned about my mental state when I threw caution to the wind with Bash. I never do that, and I'm thankful he wasn't some serial killer or sex trafficker. I got lucky.

"Ah, not much of a dancer?" he asks.

"Not really, but they love it. You here alone?" I ask, trying to be polite in this conversation.

"For now. I'm meeting my brother and a buddy here. They're late as usual," he says, rolling his eyes.

He's really cute and has a charming smile. I only use the term cute because he seriously looks like a boyish version of Bash. Bash is hot, handsome, gorgeous... Dang it, I need to stop thinking about him, and didn't I say I wouldn't call him by his name anymore?

"So, you're the friend that's always on time then," I observe.

He laughs. "Most of the time."

I take a quick glance back at Sierra, who is still dancing with the same guy. By dancing, I mean grinding up against him. I cringe, thinking about how she may indeed be going home with someone else tonight.

My attention quickly shifts to a lady pushing through beside me and knocking my purse to the ground under my feet. The contents of it spill out, and I groan. As I try to reach down for it, my arm knocks my water over, spilling all over the top of Jake's head, which is inches from my lap, as he leaned over to collect the contents of my purse.

"Crap! I'm so sorry," I say as I wipe the back of his hair with my hand.

His forehead is now literally touching my lap as I push his head down to continue wiping the water off it. I'm panicking, not knowing what to do, and this is so awkward, but it gets even more awkward as he gets yanked up off his chair by another man. No, not another man, Bash.

"What the hell is going on?" Bash, dang it, I mean, Mr. Hale asks through gritted teeth.

Jake lets out a loud laugh, and I notice everyone staring because of the commotion. Ugh, why am I so clumsy and awkward? Why does this stuff always happen to me? Why is Mr. Hale here and why is he holding the back of Jake's shirt?!

Then it all clicks. Oh! He must be Jake's brother that he was meeting here. That makes so much sense why they look alike.

Mr. Hale looks like he's two seconds away from punching his brother in the face, so I stand quickly to diffuse the situation, but I slip on the water and fall backward. A strong arm reaches out and catches me before I can hit the floor. I'm pulled back up and steadied against a muscular chest. Mr. Hale's chest.

I look up, blushing. "Uh, thank you."

I look toward Jake, who's standing with his back against the bar, watching this whole thing with amusement. This isn't funny!

"I'm so sorry Jake," I start and then look toward Mr. Hale, "my purse fell, and Jake was trying to help me pick it up, but I knocked my water all over his head... I was trying to dry it and... well... you see what happened."

Mr. Hale's gaze softens as he looks at me, and his entire demeanor changes. I stare into his eyes, and I find… amusement? Ugh. I know I'm blushing now. All of this is so embarrassing, and he's still holding onto me!

A worker clears his throat beside us. We take a step back as we realize he's holding a mop and wanting to clean up the mess. Jake finishes picking up my purse and the items that spilled out of it, handing it to me. I thank him as I grab it.

"Well, this was totally fun. I best be going," I look over toward Jake, "it was nice meeting you," then I look toward Mr. Hale, "and I'll see you at work Monday."

I run out of the building without looking back. When I get outside, I lean up against the brick wall and take a deep breath. What the heck just happened?

CHAPTER NINE

BASH

I watch Amelia race out the front door without looking back, and I'm so confused. What the fuck did I just walk into?

I stare at Jake, who has the largest grin on his face, just like he always does. His hair is dripping wet, and he's leaning against the bar, watching me. I close my eyes for a second and take a deep breath. I'll deal with him later. Right now, I need to make sure that Amelia is okay.

I run after her. When I exit the bar, I find her leaning against the building, looking like she's beating herself up about something. Is she embarrassed?

I walk up beside her. "Hey."

She gives me a weak smile. "Hey."

"So, I see you met my brother, Jake." I try to get her mind off whatever just happened in there.

She laughs. "Yeah, I did. He looks just like you. It makes sense."

"Are you here alone?" I ask with a weird pang in my chest.

What is this feeling for? Thinking about her being here with another guy makes my stomach churn. When I'm around her, I get all sorts of weird feelings, including wanting to punch my brother in the face. When I walked in and saw his head in her lap and her holding onto him, I almost lost it. I don't know what I thought was happening, but I needed to get him away from her. Was I really jealous of my brother? Amelia isn't even mine.

"Sierra wanted me to come out with her tonight. She's still inside dancing with someone," she replies.

"Don't let us be the reason you leave. Let's go back inside," I say, hoping she'll want to come back in with me.

She looks me over for a minute and says, "That's okay. I was ready to head out anyway. It was good seeing you, Mr. Hale."

I internally groan. "Please call me Bash."

She shakes her head. "You're my boss. It's Mr. Hale."

As much as I want to argue with her about my name, I don't. In fact, using my name like that makes me hard. If she looked down right now, she'd see what it does to me.

I shake those thoughts out of my head. "Do you need a ride home?"

"No, that's okay. I'm going to just text Sierra that I'm grabbing an Uber."

She pulls out her phone and starts texting, then she pulls up her Uber app.

"I don't mind driving you home," I state.

"It's not far, really. I already ordered the Uber, thank you though. Jake is probably waiting for you," she says, hinting at me to leave her alone.

Fuck if I'm going to do that. I'm not leaving her alone in the middle of New York City outside of a bar. I don't even want to let her get into the Uber, but I'll be taking a picture of the license plate when it arrives and ensure that she made it home safely.

"I'll wait with you."

She doesn't say anything to that and just looks straight ahead and then back to her phone like she's watching exactly where the Uber is. She's avoiding me, and I need to fix this between us.

"Amelia... Do you want to get coffee with me one morning?" I ask, and she looks up at me, surprised.

"Um... Like as a date or for work?" she asks.

I chuckle. "A date."

She looks back and forth between my eyes and takes a moment before answering. "I think it's best if we keep our relationship professional, Mr. Hale."

By the way she's looking at me and her breathing, I can tell she wants anything but that. I lean closer into her space with my arm against the wall above her head. Her breath hitches.

"I think we are way past keeping this relationship professional."

She's blushing at my words, and I know she's thinking about that day we were in bed together. It was magnificent.

"That was before I worked for you..." she whispers.

I shrug. "So?"

She straightens herself out and has more confidence as she says, "So that'd be unprofessional, and I need to concentrate on my job right now."

Her turning me down hurts, but I'm not going to stop trying. Unless, of course, she tells me to.

I bring my face closer to hers. "I don't care about professionalism. I want to get to know you. Unless you don't want that."

She stares at me and says nothing.

"Tell me to leave you alone, and I'll leave you alone."

She still doesn't say anything.

I smirk and step back as her Uber pulls up. "Good, then I'll text you later to confirm our coffee date."

She checks her phone to look at the number on the Uber and then walks over to it. I open the door for her to get in.

She slides in as I say, "Have a good night, Miss Hart."

"Mr. Hale." She nods at me as I close the door.

I watch her drive away with a stupid grin on my face. She didn't object to the coffee date, and she didn't tell me to stop pursuing her. That's a win.

I head back into the bar to find my brother and Ben drinking a beer. I sit in the seat next to Jake, who immediately turns to look at me.

"Did she get off safely?" he asks with that stupid knowing smirk.

"Yep," I state, waving down the bartender.

I order my drink, then Ben interrupts, "Who?"

Jake answers for me, "Amelia. A girl Bash is banging."

Ben looks at me and I glare at Jake. "I'm not banging her. I'm trying to get her to go on a date with me."

"Doesn't she work for you?" Jake questions.

"Yes."

He cocks an eyebrow. "What happened to not dating or screwing your employees?"

I shake my head. "I met her before she worked for me."

"Ah, so she banged you to get the job. Go, girl." He laughs and takes a sip of his beer.

I groan. "She didn't bang me to get the job! I met her on my work vacation. She went with another employee."

"So, you didn't bang her?" Ben chimes in.

I literally face palm my forehead. "I didn't... I mean, we slept together once, but it wasn't like that. Whatever, shut up."

I chug my beer and they both laugh, thankfully taking the hint and dropping the subject. The rest of the night, we catch up on what's been going on in the past month in our lives. We try to get the three of us together at least once a month. Sometimes it doesn't happen. It used to be the four of us when James and Jake were still friends. I miss those days, and I hope one day James will forgive my brother. Though, with the reaction I just had with Jake when I saw him with Amelia, I wouldn't blame him if he didn't.

I watch Ben as he talks and realize he looks a little more carefree than normal. Maybe it's because he's grown out his blonde hair a little, which looks similar to Jake's style. His piercing blue eyes don't look as tired as they normally do.

"Hey," a familiar voice appears beside me.

I look over to find Sierra smiling down at me. "Hey," I reply.

"So, you scared off my friend tonight, huh?"

I shake my head. "I didn't do anything."

She laughs. "It just so happened that the moment you walk in here, she walks out?"

I groan and become irritated. "I didn't want her to leave, and I would've left her alone if she stayed and wanted that."

She has a gleam in her eye. "But you wouldn't have wanted to leave her alone?"

"What is everyone's obsession with my love life?" I ask under my breath.

"Are you interested in her?" She looks serious now.

I nod. "I like her."

She went from playful, to serious, to concerned. "I'm not going to stop you, but I want you to know that she just got out of a fucked-up relationship. I don't want her to get hurt again."

Fucked-up relationship? "What happened?"

She shakes her head. "I can't tell you that. If she wants to open up to you, then she will, but it's not my place. Just... Don't hurt her. If you're not serious about her, then just walk away now."

With that, she walks off. What was that? I know they are close, and Amelia is currently living with her, but still. I try to move on and enjoy the rest of the night, but now all I can think

about is Amelia and wonder what Sierra meant by fucked-up
relationship.

CHAPTER TEN

AMELIA

The next morning, I wake to a text from Mr. Hale.

He didn't waste any time asking me on that coffee date. While I'm not sure if I should go, I can't help but smile at his text. I really should keep things professional with him, but a part of me wants to throw caution to the wind again. He makes me feel things I haven't felt in a while.

His text comes immediately after.

He doesn't say anything else, and I'm wondering if he knows where I live. I guess he could just find it in my employee file. That's technically illegal, isn't it? Would I even care if that's what he did?

I shake my head and force myself to get out of bed. I don't have any plans today, so I figured I would just relax and maybe do a little shopping with Sierra for some work clothes. She insisted I get some new clothes for the job. I'm not sure if it's because my clothes are cheap looking or if she just thinks I deserve it as a treat. I have a feeling it's the former because most of my clothes are from goodwill. She's not a snob, but I know she got me this job, so her reputation is on the line.

When I come out of the bathroom from getting ready, I run into Sierra.

"Did you want to go shopping today?" she asks.

I'm startled because I really wasn't expecting her to be awake yet. "Yeah, sure."

She laughs. "What? Did I scare you?"

"Yes! I didn't expect you up yet. Actually, I didn't even expect you to be home. I thought you'd be going home with that guy last night."

She shakes her head. "You know I don't do that. He could've been a serial killer. And even if I wanted to, Bash was there. I couldn't let my boss see me going home with a random guy."

I shrug my shoulders. "He's your boss at work, not in your personal life. He shouldn't have a say in what you do."

She gives a small smile. "He wouldn't have cared, but I don't want him thinking less of me when we work so closely."

Yeah, I feel the same way. In fact, that's a huge reason I don't want to date him. I don't like the idea of him getting to know me and judging me. It would be a lot easier just keeping it professional and only getting to know our work personalities.

We walk to the kitchen, where she pours me a cup of coffee to go. I add in creamer and sugar while she gets her own.

"Tell me about you and Bash," she says.

I roll my eyes. "There's nothing going on between us."

"That's not what he said," she says.

What? Did he tell her something?

She shakes her head and continues, "No, he didn't say anything. Though he did say he'd like to get to know you better."

"He asked me on a coffee date."

"I knew it!" She's so excited that she basically throws her coffee. "What did you say?"

"I said no at first, but... he can be pretty convincing."

She laughs. "Uh, yeah. You don't become the CEO of a successful company without being convincing... and good looking."

"We're going tomorrow."

"Do you need a ride?" she asks as she's getting even more excited.

"No, he said he'll pick me up."

"Wow, he really does like you."

I roll my eyes again. "He doesn't even know me."

"Well, he's about to get to know you. Alright, let's go."

We head out the door and to her car. I have no idea where she's taking me to go shopping, but I figured I'd let her pick. I don't know anything around here, so she's in charge today.

We make it to the first store, and I immediately ask Sierra to leave. She refuses and insists I at least try on a few outfits she picks out for me. I do as she says, but there's no way I'm buying any of these.

The first outfit is a navy-blue pencil skirt and a white blouse with a ruffle down the front. It's professional and looks amazing on me. It shows off my curves perfectly and doesn't make me look frumpy. The problem is the two pieces together cost $450. I know that I'm making some decent money, but I can't imagine spending that much on two pieces of clothing. That's like the price of a whole new wardrobe!

I come out to show Sierra and she's clapping her hands with a large grin on her face. "That's a winner!"

I shake my head and whisper, "It looks great, but I can't afford this."

She waves her hand, dismissing me. "Nonsense. It goes on the company card."

"What?" I ask surprised. She didn't relay this information to me before getting here.

She shrugs her shoulders. "Bash said to let you buy a few outfits for work. It's on him."

"Why would he do that?"

She just stares at me like I should know the answer.

"I'm not spending his money," I say.

"Amelia... he's a billionaire. He won't miss it."

My eyes go wide. "Is he really? I figured he had a lot of money, but billionaire? His company does that well?"

She shrugs her shoulders. "I think he had a lot of it before the company, but yeah, it does well."

"Either way, I'm not spending his money. I barely know the guy," I say.

"And he's trying to get to know you. So, use the money, Amelia. Get a few outfits for this job that you can also wear for teaching. You won't be making as much when you go back to teaching, so take advantage now."

What she says does make sense, but I find it difficult to use other people's hard earned money. Especially when it's an ungodly amount. I sigh and finally give in as she keeps pushing. At least it's for something I need. When I'm done wearing them, I'll donate them so someone else can get good use out of the outfits.

"Alright, let's see what else you picked for me," I say as she keeps the grin on her face and pushes me back into the fitting room.

Three thousand dollars later, professional work outfits, and a cute dress for my coffee date tomorrow, my wardrobe is ready to go. I've never had clothes this expensive or fancy before. The life that some people live is unfathomable to me. I can't imagine going to the store and just buying clothes like this on a daily basis.

My parents aren't exactly poor, but they've always lived paycheck to paycheck. They weren't able to help me pay for college, so I've been stuck with a stupid amount of student loan debt. I don't blame them for it, but I wish they would've helped me at least a little with food or something. I know they claim to love me, but sometimes I wonder how true that is. There were days that I literally didn't have food, and they just never checked in on me. They were always so busy with their own lives.

I shake my head to clear the depressing thoughts. It's all in the past, and I'm working hard to make my own way. I know Sierra will always have my back, but I need to ensure that I get myself on my feet as soon as possible. I can't rely on her forever, and I don't want to.

As I plop down on my bed after a long day of shopping, my phone dings with a text.

Mr. Hale

I hope you had fun shopping with Sierra today.

I catch myself smiling at the phone. While I'm not happy about the handout, it seems like he's happy I took it.

I did. Thank you for the new work clothes.

Mr. Hale

I can't wait to see them.

Butterflies appear in my stomach. Is he... flirting with me?

I can't wait to show you. I'll be wearing one I bought tomorrow.

Mr. Hale

Good. I was worried you'd cancel our coffee date.

Why?

I don't know why I insist on still calling him Mr. Hale when I know we've already crossed the line when it comes to being professional. I wasn't lying when I said I was overthinking tomorrow. I went back and forth about fifty times to see if I should call it off or not. In the end, I realized I would regret it if I didn't go on this date with him. It is just coffee, after all.

CHAPTER ELEVEN

BASH

I take my tie on and off twenty times before finally tossing it to the side and unbuttoning the top of my shirt. I want to look good for my date this morning, but I don't want to look like her boss. I noticed she still insists on calling me Mr. Hale. I'm hoping to remedy that today.

There's a sharp knock on my front door before it opens. I know it's Wells without even looking in his direction. He's the only one who has the balls to enter without waiting for my acknowledgement. He's the only one, besides my brother, allowed to do so. He leans against the wall, watching me.

"Can I help you?" I ask as I run my hand through my hair one more time.

He smirks. "You really like her."

It's a statement, and it's not meant to tease me. I like Wells, but I don't often let him in on my personal life, at least, of what he doesn't need to know.

"I think I do," I state.

He nods. "If you want to pick her up on time, we should head out."

He pushes off the wall, and I follow behind him to the elevator. Wells is a good guy and someone I trust with my life. He just turned forty, and he doesn't have a family of his own, which is surprising. He's good looking. He has some gray starting to pepper his brown hair and clean-shaven. He has brown eyes, though not many know that considering he's usually wearing sunglasses, even inside. I stare at him as we ride down the elevator and notice the wrinkles on his face.

He notices me staring. "What?"

I chuckle. "Nothing. Just noticing how this job is aging you."

"Thanks…" he states.

I shake my head. He's damn good at his job. Being ex-military, he knows how to fight and can see a threat from a mile away. He doesn't stick with me 24/7 like some of my friends' security does. I can take care of myself, but being a billionaire puts a target on your back. He typically drives and comes with me to big meetings or events where there will be a lot of people. I'll often have him drive me to and from work, so I can get things done on the way. Plus, driving in New York isn't my favorite thing to do.

I have him with me today as a precaution. I like Amelia and going out with her could put a target on her back. I want to make sure I have him watching out for anyone suspicious. Plus, I feel like the sooner she meets him, the better.

We pull up to Sierra's apartment complex. I tell Wells to wait out here for us while I buzz up to Sierra's apartment.

"I'll be right down," the voice over the intercom says.

Well, I was hoping she'd buzz me in, but I guess I can wait here for her. It takes about five minutes for her to come down, but the moment I spot her makes it worth the wait. She's in a knee length floral dress that fits tight against her waist. Her red hair is wavy and let down today. She has on a bit of makeup, but I can still see the little freckles that line her cheeks and the top of her nose. So. Fucking. Beautiful.

"Hey," she says as she stops in front of me shyly.

"Hey," I breathe out.

She looks up at me through her lashes with her head still down. She lacks confidence, but I'm going to change that.

"You look beautiful, Amelia," I state.

She gives a small smile back. "Thank you."

I can tell by the way she replies she doesn't believe me. That's okay, I'll tell her as many times as she needs me to for her to understand it's true.

I lead her to the SUV and open the back door for her. She looks confused for a moment but enters the car and I shut the door. I round the car and jump in on the other side. She's already talking to Wells as he clearly introduced himself to her.

She looks over at me. "I didn't know you had a driver."

I smile. Of course he introduced himself as my driver. "It depends if I feel like driving or not, but Wells isn't just my driver.

He's the head of my security and can take out a guy in five seconds flat if needed."

I watch her as she processes what I just told her. I don't know if I should've kept some of this for a later time, but I don't want to mess around with her. I don't like when things come out later and cause issues.

"That makes sense," she whispers as she looks out the window.

I hope I'm not scaring her off already.

I don't say anything else as I watch her stare out the window. She sits with her hands fidgeting on her lap and occasionally her leg bounces up and down, but she stops herself and then she does it again. I can't help the smile that creeps up on my face as I watch her. She's nervous.

It's a silent and awkward ride to the coffee shop, but it only took about ten minutes to get there. I thought about putting her out of her misery a few times and starting a conversation, but I don't mind the silence and just being in her presence. I also wanted to see how she interacts with these types of situations. Which clearly, she's not one that fills silence with idle talk like most girls I have gone out with in the past. Honestly, it's refreshing.

Wells pulls over at the coffee shop. I get out on the street side and round the back of the car. By the time I'm around the car, she has gotten out as well. She's independent and not going to wait for a man to open her door. I'm thinking she has never had a man in her life before that would that.

I close the door and pin her up against the side of the car. "Let me open the door for you next time."

She swallows and stares at me before nodding. She's uncomfortable, but I don't think she minds being told what to do. I inwardly groan, thinking about what that may look like in the bedroom. I quickly erase those thoughts and put some distance between us. Placing my lower hand on her back, I lead her into the coffee shop, after opening the door for her, of course.

There's no line, so we step right up. She orders the same thing as the last time she got coffee, a hot white chocolate mocha. The smallest cup size. I order my usual black coffee. I don't drink fancy coffee.

We step to the side to wait for our orders. We're standing in awkward silence again, but this time it doesn't take long for her to fill it.

She looks up at me. "So you like to drink mud, got it."

I laugh. "It doesn't taste like mud."

She has the most gorgeous smile. "I'm pretty sure black coffee tastes like mud. That's okay, we all have our preferences. I don't judge."

"Sounds a little like judging."

This time she laughs. "Not at all. I just figured it's good to know what my boss drinks in case I need to bring him a coffee."

"That's my assistant's job," I state.

"What about your girlfriend's?" she asks. Her eyes immediately go wide as she realizes what she just asked.

"Do you want to be my girlfriend?" I ask, watching her closely for her reaction.

Her cheeks turn red, and she looks to the ground. Adorable.

I grab her chin to look up at me. "I wouldn't be opposed. That's why I asked you on a date, so we can get to know each other better."

Oddly, that's true. When I met her on vacation, I had no intention of getting into a relationship. I've been content focusing on my company as it's growing rapidly. Amelia is different, though. I still don't know what it is about her, but I can't seem to stay away.

She just nods, and the barista calls her name. She bolts from my grip on her and grabs her coffee. Mine quickly follows, and we sit by the window. She looks out of it, watching the people walk by. I can tell she's thankful for the distraction, but I want her attention all on me right now.

"So, why did you decide to move all the way from California to New York?" I ask to get her attention.

She snaps her head in my direction. "There were a few reasons, but mainly because this is where Sierra lives."

"You wanted to move closer to your best friend?" I look at her curiously. I know there's more to the story than that.

She shrugs her shoulders.

I place my hand on hers. "Hey, if you don't want to tell me, that's fine, but I want to get to know you. I'm a pretty straightforward guy."

She nods and says, "Honestly, I needed to escape my past. I got dealt with a crappy hand a few months back with losing my job, and I ended things with my ex shortly after. I thought it would be nice to have a fresh start away from everything."

"What about your parents?" I ask.

She shrugs again. "We get along fine, but they are just busy with their own lives. I get it. I don't think they ever really wanted kids as I was an accident, so once I left for college, I was no longer their problem."

For once, I'm at a loss on what to say. I don't know her well enough to know how what I want to say would be taken. Regardless, she shouldn't feel like a fucking problem. It doesn't take a scientist to figure out that she feels like an inconvenience to everyone around her. I clocked that two seconds after meeting her.

"Amelia... You're amazing. You're not someone's problem. I hope you never feel like that around me." I want to say so much more, but I keep it to myself.

She gives me that small smile. "Thanks... So, what about you? I know you have your brother and aren't close to your parents either, but have you lived in New York your whole life?"

"Yeah. We grew up here. Most of my friends and family are still here. What about you? Do you have friends back where you used to live?" I ask, trying to get a better read on her. I don't want to be selfish, but I'm hoping she says no, so she doesn't have any more ties there.

"I lived in San Diego, and nah. We all drifted apart after..." she clears her throat, "Sierra was the only one that stuck it out with me."

"What do you mean?"

She looks out the window for a moment and back to me. "Honestly, my ex wasn't a good guy. He isolated me from everyone, and I let him."

"He was abusive," I state.

It doesn't need to be a question. I know the type. I've met many of them. They control you by isolating you from friends and family. Then they belittle you and make you feel like you're not worth anything, which clearly is how she still feels. Sometimes it ends there, but other times...

"Did he ever hurt you?" I ask, gritting my teeth.

She looks out the window again and doesn't respond.

"Amelia," I say in a stern voice.

She looks back at me and nods.

Fuck.

"Not at first," she looks around before continuing, "but toward the end, yeah. There were just a few times at the beginning, but he apologized and seemed so upset by his actions. He went years without doing it again, but then when I lost my job and found out he was cheating on me... things got intense. I was stupid for staying with him for so long."

I close my eyes for a moment, trying to control my rage. How could someone hurt her like that? I want to ask Wells to find the guy, but I don't know if I can control myself on what I'd do to him when I found him.

I open my eyes and see the shine to hers. She's still haunted by her past, and I can't blame her. It's been what, only a few months?

I grab her hand, and she jumps slightly from my touch. Fuck.

"Amelia... I want to make myself clear. I will never lay a hand on you and if any man ever does again, you need to tell me immediately. Understand?"

"Yes," she whispers.

"Good. Now, do you want to end our date after coffee, or would you like to go for a walk?" I ask, hoping she'll choose the latter.

She smiles. "A walk sounds amazing."

I stand from my seat and hold my hand out for her to take. We toss our cups on the way out the door. I didn't mean for our coffee date to go like this, but I'm glad it did. I wanted to get to know her better and wanted to know about her ex. I didn't think she'd open up so quickly to me. Maybe I'm not the only one feeling this odd connection between us.

Chapter Twelve

AMELIA

It's Friday again, and this week has flown by. I'm not as exhausted as I was at this point last week, but I'm still pretty tired. Sierra has me running around like crazy, and I forgot my coffee on the way out the door this morning. I've only been at work for two hours, and I feel like I need a nap.

I lay my head on my desk, just to rest my eyes for a few minutes. Whenever I get a free moment, I can't help but think about Mr. Hale and our date the other morning. I can't believe I actually told him about my past. Not even Sierra knows much about my ex. She knows enough, and I know she's guessed, but I've never confirmed he was actually abusive toward me.

We spent hours walking around New York and getting to know each other better. He seems to genuinely want to get to know me. I'm shocked considering how we started out. We both just had a physical attraction to each other, which we acted on. I really thought that was the end of us, but I'm thankful it's not.

I'm still wary around guys, but there's just something different about him.

It's also hard whenever I go into his office and see him in his suit. We agreed to always keep things professional at work. It's not that we're necessarily hiding our relationship, but I think it's best not to cross the line while here. Oh how I wish he'd cross that line every time I walk into his office. I might be wearing that tight navy pencil skirt today in hopes of torturing him a little. He seems to have no problem keeping his cool though, or maybe he's really not that interested in me...

I startle as I hear a thud on my desk. I lift my head to find Mr. Hale smiling down at me, and I'm embarrassed. He rarely comes to my desk. Why did he have to the one time I had my head down?!

"Uh, I was just..." I say, but trail off when I see what was placed on my desk.

"You looked a little tired, so I thought this would help," he states, pushing the coffee closer to me.

I take a sip and realize it's the white chocolate mocha that I always order. I close my eyes and savor how good it tastes, especially since I didn't get to drink my coffee this morning.

"Thank you so much. I forgot my coffee at home, so I haven't had any yet today," I state while taking another sip.

"You're welcome. I could use your help with something at eleven if you don't mind coming to my office," he states.

"Uh yeah, sure. I'll see you at eleven. Thank you again."

He stares at me for a moment before walking off. That was... really nice of him. I've never had anyone bring me coffee before or really consider any of my needs. Well, besides Sierra. I'm thankful for her, but it's nice to have a guy do it for once.

Because I can't be happy for too long, my brain forces me back into another memory of my ex.

"I'm going to grab a coffee. I'll be back in a bit," Jay says while pulling his coat on at the front door.

I place my pen down and look up at him. I've been studying for hours, and I'm exhausted.

"Do you mind grabbing me one too?"

"Yeah, what do you want?" he asks and puts his boots on.

"Just my usual," I state and pick my pen up again.

He huffs. "What is that?"

I laugh and look up at him. The laughter quickly fades when I realize he's serious and now looking angry.

"Huh?" I ask, confused because he can't be asking me what my usual is.

"The coffee you want. What is it?"

"My usual," I repeat.

"Yeah, well, you gotta give me more than that. What's your usual?" he asks seriously again.

"Really? The same thing I get every time we get coffee," I say, getting annoyed.

"Well sometimes you get something different, so just tell me what you want or I'm not getting it," he says, heading toward the door.

"A white chocolate mocha... and no... I never get anything else," I say, but try to keep my attitude in check. I don't want to start an argument.

He rolls his eyes. "Whatever. If I remember, I'll bring you a coffee."

He slams the door on his way out, and I place my head on the table, annoyed. Ugh. How can he not know what my usual coffee is? I've been getting the same thing for like five years. Yeah, I don't get it every day, but I feel like after the first, like, ten times, he should know what type of coffee I drink.

I shake my head, trying to get out of my thoughts. Now I'm annoyed all over again. Those are the red flags that I should've caught onto and ended our relationship a lot sooner. The kicker was, he brought back my white chocolate mocha, but it was iced. I never get iced.

I take another sip of my coffee and smile. Yeah, this is how it should be. I never knew what I was missing until Mr. Hale came into my life. I relax in my chair and enjoy the coffee, thinking about the handsome billionaire who has been on my mind day and night.

It's fifteen minutes past eleven, and I'm late getting to Mr. Hale's office. I hope he's not angry with me. Sierra's meeting went over, and I was needed in there to help take notes because her other assistant went home sick today.

I knock on the door, and he tells me to come in. I open it and quickly close it behind me.

"I'm so sorry I'm late. Sierra's meeting went over," I state and notice he's staring at me.

I'm not sure what that look is. He looks frustrated, but not mad. I hate being late and inconveniencing people.

He clears his throat. "It happens."

He picks up his phone and starts typing.

"I really am sorry. I hate being late and an inconvenience," I say.

He lifts his head to look at me. "You're not an inconvenience, Amelia. Meetings run over, it's okay."

"Then why do you seem frustrated with me?" I ask, a little frustrated myself.

"I'm not..." he pauses and runs his hand through his hair, "I'm not frustrated with you."

I place my hands on the front of his desk. "Are you sure? It's okay if you are. I understand it's my fault for being late."

He gets up from his chair so quickly it startles me, and I take a step back, turning as he rounds his desk. My butt is against the front of his desk as he pins me against it and places his hand on my cheek.

"I'm not frustrated with you, Amelia," he says softly.

I let out the breath I was holding and whisper back, "Then with what?"

He closes his eyes and takes a deep breath. "Do you want me to be honest?"

"Always," I state.

He leans over, whispering in my ear, "I'm frustrated with myself. Every time I see you in my office, I want to bend you over my desk and take you right here."

My breath catches again, and I close my eyes this time. That's exactly what I think about every time too, but I shouldn't say it. I can't say it. We're supposed to be staying professional at work. That's why I haven't been able to let myself call him Bash, or Sebastian. After finding out what his name is short for, I haven't been able to get it out of my head. I feel like it'll cross the line, and I don't know where the line is anymore, if there even is one.

"Mr. Hale..." I breathe out.

He groans.

"Mr. Hale..." I state again, but am still unable to finish my sentence. I don't even know what I'm trying to say.

"Amelia..." he says like he's at a loss for words, too.

His face is only inches from mine. We're staring at each other, both wanting the same thing, but neither of us daring to make the first move. I don't know how long we stand here for, but it feels like an eternity. If I just leaned forward a little... I could just...

Someone knocks on the door, and he jumps back, making me well aware of the situation he has going on in his pants. He clears his throat and sits down behind his desk. I take a few steps back, and he nods for me to open the door, so I do.

When I open it, I find Sierra on the other side. I don't know whether I want to thank her or hit her for interrupting us, but I know it's for the best. If she hadn't knocked on the door, I would've broken the distance between us and kissed him. Then I would've let him bend me over his desk and take me. That is not something I need to do at work.

"Oh! I didn't mean to interrupt..." Sierra says with a grin on her face.

I step to the side as Mr. Hale says, "You're not interrupting. Amelia finished helping me. Thank you."

I nod. "You're welcome."

I walk out the door without another word or glancing at Sierra. I know she's looking at me with amusement. She knows. I know she knows.

When I make it back to my desk, I realize he never told me why he asked me to his office in the first place. I think about texting him to ask if I should come back later but decide against it. I have a feeling we need to keep our distance for the rest of the day, or I'll end up naked across his desk.

Chapter Thirteen

BASH

Fuck me. My restraint when it comes to Amelia is fading. She's worn a different outfit every day this week, and each one is more torturous than the other. I don't remember who came up with the rule to stay professional at work, but I'm regretting agreeing to it every damn day.

When I saw her pencil skirt and low-cut blouse today, I lost it. It was even worse seeing how grateful she was for me bringing her a simple cup of coffee. She acted like it was a diamond necklace I gave her. Has no one ever brought her something so simple as coffee before?

Regardless, I've wanted to bend her over my desk every damn day. I don't know what I was thinking, inviting her to my office earlier today. I didn't have a reason to, other than to just see her again and apparently torture myself. It's a good thing Sierra interrupted us because I know exactly where we would've ended up if she hadn't.

I pack up my laptop and throw the bag over my shoulder. I don't usually leave work this early, but I'm having an early dinner with a good friend, Timothy Odier. I just call him Tim, but I'm the only one allowed to. We met in college and have been in business together since I've started my company. He uses us for financial help, and I'm thankful he trusted me to work with his company.

He's waiting for me when I exit the building.

"Hey man!" He grabs my hand, pulling me in for a hug and shoulder pat.

"Hey, I thought we were meeting at the restaurant," I state.

His grin widens. "I thought I'd pick you up in my new ride."

Oh no. He always has a new ride, and it's usually something ridiculous. It always matches his frat boy personality and looks. You can typically find him wearing pastel color suits with sunglasses and a hat with his shaggy, dirty blonde hair sticking out. Underneath those sunglasses are sometimes his natural dark brown eyes, but he often likes to wear blue contact lenses.

I search the cars as we pass by. I wonder what it'll be this time. We continue to walk a few more cars down, and then I spot it. Yep, that has to be his.

"Seriously man?" I ask, shaking my head.

"Isn't she perfect?!" he asks, leading me over to the ridiculous-looking car.

Or should I say, truck? Or, I don't even know. It's one of those weird-looking Cybertrucks that looks like it's from the future. I know I'm rich, but I've never been one to have fancy cars. Don't get me wrong, my cars are expensive, but they're practical. I can't see how this is practical.

"How do you even open the door?" I ask, staring at it like a handle will magically appear on the car.

He pulls out his phone and taps a button, making the car light up and his door opens. Wait, what? I shake my head. Whatever...

"Bash..." A familiar deep voice rumbles behind me.

I turn around to find my father standing next to me. He's not usually on this side of New York, so I'm curious what he's doing here.

"Hey, dad. What brings you here?" I ask.

"I just came from a meeting down the street. Leaving work early today?" he asks in a condescending tone.

"Bash, we're going to be late for our meeting, so make it quick," Tim says as he enters his ridiculous Cybertruck and closes the door.

This is why I love the guy. Not that I need him to stick up for me in front of my father, but he does without asking. He's one of the most loyal friends you can have. We went through a lot of crap together in college and the beginning stages of our companies, but we made it through. Together.

"Sorry, he's right. I don't want to be late," I state, about to turn away when he stops me again.

"Have you talked to Jake recently?" he asks with a weird note in his voice.

"What do you mean?"

"I'm... concerned about him," he states without elaborating.

"Concerned how?"

He shakes his head. "He's just... Jake. I've been hearing rumors, and I think he just needs to grow up a little. Be more like you."

Well, that's... a compliment? My father doesn't give out compliments often, so I'm surprised, but I don't want one that throws my brother under the bus.

"He's doing great, dad. He's smart, and he's never screwed up," I say, but I know that's not true.

He's never screwed up that my father has seen. I've bailed him out of many situations before my father had to get involved or even know about it.

"You and I both know that's not true, son."

Well, maybe he does know about some of them. Regardless, Jake is a great guy, and he's professional when he needs to be. He gets the job done. He may have a little more fun than most people, but he's not dumb. Well... when he went to jail in Costa Rica and I had to bail him out, that was pretty dumb.

"What's your real question?" I ask, getting annoyed.

If he wants to talk about Jake, then he needs to have these conversations with him. Then again, I'm pretty sure he has been, and they've fallen on deaf ears.

"He needs to settle down and find himself a wife. Make some roots," he states.

I laugh. "What do you want me to do about that? He hasn't found the right woman yet, and that's not his fault."

"He's stuck on a woman he'll never have. I just... I was hoping you could try to talk some sense into him," he states, looking at the ground and back up at me.

My heart clenches at how he looks. He really does look concerned and like... he cares about Jake. I know he cares about both of us, but he never shows it. Jake's right, there's something going on with dad.

"Are you alright?" I ask with concern in my own voice.

He clears his throat. "Of course. It's just time for your brother to settle down and take this business seriously. I won't be around forever, and he needs to take over. Preferably with a wife by his side and some heirs."

I have no idea what is going on with the old man, but I decide to throw him a bone. "Alright, yeah. I'll talk to him."

"Thanks, son," he says with a pat on my shoulder.

"See you around," I say as I round the car and try to figure out how I get into this damn thing.

The car door pops open, and I open it wide to get in before I hear my dad yell, "Let's make dinner plans soon with your mom."

I nod and get into the car. Tim raises his eyes at me like he's asking if I'm ready. I close the door to indicate I am, and he drives off. I shake off the odd encounter with my dad and focus on the ridiculous car we're driving in.

"What was that about?" Tim asks.

"I have no idea," I whisper back, lost in my thoughts again.

We sit at our usual table when we arrive at the restaurant. This is where we come whenever we just need some friend time or when we need to talk business. Tonight is friend time, and I'm thankful for it. I could use a friend to talk to about Amelia.

"You go first. What's new in your life?" he asks.

I can't help the smile that grows on my face as I think about Amelia.

"Ah, there's a girl," he states with a grin.

"Yeah, it's complicated though. We met on vacation and slept together once. Then she became my employee," I state.

Tim chokes on his water and starts laughing. "Did you know she applied for the job when you slept with her?"

"Of course not. She applied after, but she didn't know who I was either. Like I said, it's complicated," I say.

"Do you want more with her?" he asks.

I don't even need to think before responding, "Yes."

He shrugs his shoulders. "Doesn't sound too complicated to me. Give it a try. If it doesn't work out, move her to another department."

He makes it sound so easy, but it's not since she's Sierra's best friend and assistant. "I can't just screw her on the job."

Tim laughs again. "Are you kidding? That's the best part about having a relationship with someone at work. Random breaks, banging on the desk, below the desk blow jobs... Need I say more?"

I groan, thinking about Amelia on her knees by my desk giving me a blow job. Ugh, I didn't even think about that one.

I've been fantasizing all the ways I could have her bent over my desk, but now that'll be an added fantasy.

"I take it you've done all those things." I state, not ask.

He grins and takes another drink of his water. The waitress interrupts us to take our orders, then leaves us alone to continue our conversation.

"I don't want to ruin things with her. She wants to keep it professional between us at work," I say.

He taps his fingers on the table. "Alright, I can see the problem. You sure she wouldn't be open to it? How long have you two been going out?"

"We've only been on one date."

He laughs. "Oh man. I give it until next week and you'll be screwing her on your desk. Just give it time."

I shake my head and need a topic change. Maybe he's not the best person to talk to about my relationship with Amelia. This conversation might be best with James.

"So, tell me about you. Anyone in your life?" I ask, but I know the answer.

"Nah. Just having fun like always," he says, averting his gaze from me.

He's been in love with his best friend's sister since he was eighteen, probably even sooner. They grew up together and apparently, she only looks at him as an older brother. I don't blame her, though. He acts like an older brother. I don't think he's ever told her how he feels. He doesn't want to cross the line with her and definitely doesn't want to ruin his relationship with his best friend.

I don't push him to talk about her anymore, so I move on. "Work's good?"

"Things are going great. We had a security breach in our system about a month ago, but it's taken care of now," he states as our food arrives.

"Interesting. We had one too about that same time," I say, wondering if they are related to one another.

"That's coincidental. Did you find out who?" he asks.

"Not yet. They covered their tracks well."

"Same," he states, cutting into his medium-rare steak.

"How's Jake?" he asks, going through our usual conversation pieces.

"He's... Jake, but he's good."

Tim laughs. "Yeah, I don't ever see him growing up. Honestly, I wish I was more like him sometimes. Life's too short. We should be having fun."

He's not wrong. There are times I wish I could be as carefree as my little brother, but I do know better. It's mostly a show for everyone else. While he does have fun, I know there's a lot that he's hiding from everyone.

We finish the night catching up and laughing. I never realize how much I need a night like tonight with my friend until I have it. I'm always so focused on work, I need to learn to take more time for myself.

CHAPTER FOURTEEN

AMELIA

Things have been going really well with Bash. Yes, I'm calling him Bash now, at least, outside of work. There is no more line. While we've kept it mostly professional at work, I've been avoiding being alone in his office as much as I can. He seems to respect that decision.

We've been out on two more dates. The first we went to see a movie and the second we went out to dinner. He hasn't once pressured me to sleep with him again, but he has kissed me good night after each date. He holds the door open for me and pulls out my seat wherever we go. We hold hands, and he's the perfect gentleman. And we text. A lot.

He texts me every single morning and night, along with throughout the day, whenever he's thinking about me. Not a day goes by that he doesn't text me something along the lines of "good morning, beautiful" or "good night, gorgeous." He'll often just throw in something telling me how wonderful I am and that he's lucky to be able to spend time with me.

He's the complete opposite of my ex. Bash wants to spend time with me. I used to have to beg my ex to take me out on a simple coffee date or to watch a movie at home. We lived together for so many years and yet, we barely saw each other. If I got desperate enough to hang out with him, I'd make sure to plan something that he really wanted to do, even if I wouldn't enjoy it.

My ex didn't know anything about me. He couldn't tell you what my favorite color or favorite animal was. He wouldn't be able to tell you what I did with my time or even what classes I was taking. He didn't care, but Bash... Bash cares. He wants to know every little thing about me, and I'm pretty sure he now knows. If we don't talk about it on dates, then we're talking about it through texts. I believe he has a photographic memory or something because he remembers everything that I tell him about myself.

Speaking of Bash... I look at my phone to find a text from him.

Bash

Can you come to my office?

Be there in five.

My heart beats faster as I think about what he could want. He rarely texts me to come to his office. Usually if he needs something, it comes through Sierra, since I'm her assistant. This must be something personal, and I'm nervous about that. What does he want?

I hit the bathroom before heading to his office just to kill a little time and calm my nerves. I swipe my hands down the sides of my dress to flatten out any creases that may be there. Taking a deep breath, I knock on his door.

"Come in," he says from the other side.

I open it and enter slowly, closing it behind me. "You wanted to see me, Mr. Hale?"

His eyes darken at my words, and he straightens in his chair. "Sit."

My nerves get the better of me again at his tone. Oh no, what did I do? I must have done something. My feet barely want to move, but I force them to and concentrate on putting one foot in front of the other. Apparently, concentrating on walking is a bad idea because somehow, I trip over my own feet and, in slow motion, faceplant the floor. I wish I could say I'm exaggerating, but I full on faceplant. I'm so embarrassed, I don't even want to get up. My cheek is on the cold tiled floor, while my hands are flat against it. I'm frozen.

"Amelia!" I hear Bash's voice as he races over to me.

Can I just lie here and die? Why am I so clumsy? This is so embarrassing.

Bash helps me to my feet, and I just laugh, saying, "I'm fine!"

Bash looks me over with concern in his eyes and touches my forehead. Ow, okay, maybe I did hit my head a little. I'm not going to show it though.

"You hit your head," he states seriously.

I swat his hand away. "I'm fine, really." I head to the seat in front of his desk and sit down. "So, what did you need?"

Bash takes a moment before sitting in his chair across from me, still eyeing me with concern. Okay, Bash, can we please pretend that never happened? I'm pretending, so come on.

He clears his throat. "I know you wanted to keep things professional at work, but I'm leaving for an unexpected work trip this weekend for a week. I wanted to talk to you about something..."

He looks so nervous, which is making me nervous. Which isn't a horrible thing because it's keeping my thoughts off my throbbing forehead.

"Yes?" I ask, hoping he'll continue sooner rather than later.

"I... was hoping you'd want to put a title on our relationship. I'd like to officially say you're my girlfriend... that is... if you want that?"

The smile grows on my face. I was not expecting that. What else I wasn't expecting, is to get back into a relationship so soon after breaking it off with my ex, but with Bash, this is an easy answer.

"I'd love that," I say softly.

He grins and rounds his desk in front of me. I stand to meet him as he pulls me into a kiss. A hard, passionate kiss. I moan, which is embarrassing, but I can't help myself. He pulls away, staring down at me like he wants to do more with me. So do I.

I clear my throat. "Where are you going?"

He steps back and sits on his desk in front of me. "Austin, Texas. There's an opportunity to bring on another client."

"That sounds great, but that means you won't be here for your birthday..." I state.

He shakes his head. "That's okay. We can celebrate when I get back. How did you know it was my birthday?"

I laugh. "You think I wouldn't know my boyfriend's birthday?"

"I just became your boyfriend forty seconds ago."

I shrug my shoulders. "What can I say? I work fast."

He smiles and steps back in front of me. He wraps his arms around me, pulling me in for another kiss.

"I'll miss you. I'll text every day," he says softly.

I melt into him, literally. Burying my face in his chest, I breathe him in and enjoy his embrace. I don't know how I got this lucky to find a man like him or what he sees in me, but I'm thankful. While I know I have a long way to go, he's really been helping me gain confidence in myself. He taught me that I am worth it, and I do deserve happiness. That I didn't deserve my ex abusing and cheating on me. I deserve so much more, and that's what Bash is giving me.

I step away from him to put a little distance between us. "Well Mr. Hale, I should probably get back to work."

He groans. "Mmm, I should too."

We both stare at each other, neither of us moving.

I clear my throat. "Alright... I'm... Going..."

I take a couple of steps backward and he just watches me.

"I'm heading out now… So if…" I'm stopped as a door slams into the back of my head, making me falter forward.

"Amelia!" Bash yells out in concern for a second time today.

"Shit," a voice says as he catches my arm to steady me, so I don't fall flat on my face again.

I rub the back of my head as I hear Bash yelling at his brother, Jake.

"What the hell are you doing?" Bash yells.

"Sorry, man. Your assistant said you were alone in here," Jake says while looking me over to make sure I'm alright.

"I'm sorry Amelia. Are you okay?" Jake asks with the same concern his brother has.

Man, they really look exactly alike, right down to the same facial expressions. Alright, I need to get out of here before I make a fool of myself even more.

"It's okay. Bye Bash, have a good trip." I turn to Jake and say, "It was good seeing you. Bye."

With my hand still on the back of my head, I race out the door and neither of them follow me. Thank God. I rush back toward Sierra's office and knock.

"Come in," she yells.

I barge in panting and plant myself in the seat in front of her desk.

"What happened? Is everything okay?" she asks me, concerned as well.

I realize I'm still holding the back of my head. "I'm fine. You know me, I'm clumsy. Fell on my face and then got hit with a door, it's fine."

"Do you need an icepack or something?" she asks.

I laugh. "Nope, I'm good."

We stare at each other for a minute until she finally breaks. "So, are you going to tell me why you're in here?"

"Oh... Right... So... Bash and I are official. I'm his girlfriend," I say.

Sierra stares at me for a second before the high-pitched squealing starts. I laugh and shush her at the same time. One because I don't want anyone else to hear what's going on in here, but two, my head really does hurt.

"You need to tell me the details," she says, waiting for all the gossip.

I laugh again. "Tonight. I'll tell you everything tonight."

We smile at each other, and I'm just so excited. I haven't felt this way in a long time.

CHAPTER FIFTEEN

BASH

My brother sits in front of me with guilt written on his face. "So, why are you here?"

Jake rubs the back of his head and looks toward the door. "Are you sure she's alright? I'm sorry, I didn't know anyone was in here, or I would've knocked. Should we go check on her?"

I laugh. Is that why he looks so guilty? My fucking brother. He always seems so carefree, but he really cares about others, even if he doesn't show it.

"Nah, she's fine. Trust me, she wouldn't have wanted us to follow her. It happens all the time," I say with a dumb smile on my face, thinking about how clumsy and awkward she can be.

"She gets hit with doors all the time? Why does she stand so close to them?" Jake asks, looking confused.

I laugh again. "No, she's just clumsy. Right before you came in, she fell and faceplanted the floor, tripping over her own two feet."

Jake's face relaxes into a smile. "Ah. I've met some clumsy girls before. They're cute, but can be dangerous."

Jake shivers as he's clearly thinking about a situation.

"Do I want to know?" I ask.

"No... No you don't. Anyway, I did come for a reason," Jake says.

"And that reason?" I ask.

His smile grows even more. "Guess who's back?"

I shake my head. "When did she get back?"

"A little over a month ago," he answers.

"How's she doing? Settling in?"

"She's great. She has a nice place and setup with her security team. She's grown up a lot since you've last seen her," he says.

It's been a while since I've seen Everly. I feel bad that I haven't made more of an effort to go see her the past six years she's been gone and in Georgia. Jake has seen her a lot, but I know he has feelings for her. While my texts haven't been daily, I made sure to text her at least once or more a week. It's something I started after she tried to commit suicide when she was in her senior year of high school.

She's been through a lot, and I wish there was more I could've done for her. She lost one of her close friends to suicide and she was the one to find her. Then she also had a horrible ex-boyfriend who used to rape her. He didn't want to let her go, so he caused a lot of issues in her life. Looking back at that time, I wish I would've done more to protect and help her. I hate that I didn't. If I could go back, I would do a lot of things differently, but I can't. So, I make sure that I do what I can now, which is to just let her know that she's worth it and to be here for her if she needs me.

Thinking about all this is interesting, as it reminds me of Amelia. Abusive ex and little self-worth... Is that why I'm so drawn to her? I shake my head before I think too much into this. I really like Amelia. She's beautiful, smart, and funny. We have a great time together.

"Well, I can't wait to see her again. Does James know?" I ask.

Jake rolls his eyes. "We both know the answer to that."

"Have you two cleared the air yet?"

"No. I told you that I'm done making the first move. It's on him now, but I'm not going to start anything, Bash," he says seriously.

I shake my head. "I know... It's just now that she's back, you know that you're going to be seeing him again at some point. He's not going to let her go again."

I watch for Jake's reaction. He doesn't give one.

"Sebastian, for the last time, I'm over her. She's my best friend, and that's all we'll ever be. She's meant to be with James. I know James, and he's going to make sure she realizes that. I hope they finally get their happy ending."

Jake rarely calls me by my first name unless he needs a point to get across or he's really angry with me. He's being sincere right now, and I believe him. While he says all these things, I know it still hurts him. He did love her, I know he did. In a way, I think she loved him too, but not as much as she loves James.

I nod, but don't say anything back.

Jake sits forward. "So, tell me about Amelia."

I can't help the grin that forms on my face. "She's officially my girlfriend."

Jake pumps his arm in the air. "Yeah! Finally, man. I was starting to wonder if you'd turned gay."

I laugh and shake my head. "I just hadn't found anyone worth it."

"She's beautiful and sounds like she's going to be a handful," he says.

"Yeah, she is, but I really like her. We have a good time together."

He wiggles his eyebrows with the grin on his face. "Oh yeah? So, office sex?"

I shake my head again. "Not like that. No, we haven't, not since the vacation at least. We're taking our time getting to know each other. I don't know though. I feel like this is the real deal, you know?"

His smile falters for a split second before he plasters it back on. Not many would catch it, but I do.

"Nah, not sure I do, but I'm happy for you," he says, standing up.

I stand with him. "You will, Jake."

"Yeah, sure." He pats me on the shoulder before heading toward the door.

"I'll reach out to Everly and welcome her back," I say.

Jake salutes me and walks out the door. I take a deep breath and let it out. I hate how much my brother hurts. It sounds stupid, but I think he really wants someone to love and to love him back. Someone who chooses him first and not second. I don't blame Everly for anything, as she's always been straightforward with Jake, but I just wish he could find someone.

I sit back down behind my desk and think about Everly being back. The fact that she "couldn't" get a job and only landed one back here makes me know it wasn't her fault. I know James had a hand in that, so he knows she's back in town. I'm wondering if he made his move yet.

I pull out my phone to text him.

> I heard Everly is back in town.

I place my phone down and debate if I should text Everly or not. I decide to wait until I finish my conversation with James since he just texted back.

James

> I bumped into her earlier this week.

> Bumped into huh? How'd she look?

James

> Beautiful as always.

I laugh and shake my head. Of course.

I want to get us all together, but I'm not going to push James. While Jake is over the feud between them, I know James isn't. Again, I see both sides. I don't know how I'd feel if Amelia and I took a break and her ex stepped in for a bit. I feel like I want to vomit just thinking about it. No, I know how I'd feel. I know it's a little different, but still.

Jake and Everly tried the dating thing first, but it only lasted a few days. Everly already had feelings for James and Jake was... well, Jake. Flirty and not knowing how to have a girlfriend.

So, they decided to stay friends and then eventually James and Everly became a thing. She went through a lot of crap and broke it off with James to start a new life in Georgia, away from everything. I know she did it for James, so he could concentrate on his business. He would've given it all up for her. We all know it, and so did she. That's why she did it.

A couple of years later, James was in a hard place where there was a marriage proposition. The media portrayed it like they were actually together, but they weren't. He was still waiting for Everly. She caught wind and Jake happened to be there that summer, so things happened. I don't know all the details, but I know they had a friends with benefits situation. Even though Jake will never admit it, I know he wanted more. Everly knew too, so she broke it off with him when she figured it out. He was different after that summer and hasn't been the same since. That was about four years ago.

We've all been friends since we were little kids. I hate how complicated things have become. I decide to text Everly.

> I hear you're back for good. Any reason I heard this from my brother and not you?

Her response doesn't come immediately, so I set my phone down. She knows I'm not really upset about it, but I have to tease her anyway. I finish up a few emails before she texts back.

Bush man! I'm sorry, I've been busy settling in with my new job and place.

I smile at the nickname. That was a stupid nickname she gave me back in my college days. Everly, Jake, and Ben came to visit for James' birthday while we were at college. We were stupid back then and had mixed drugs and alcohol together. It was a great time, until it wasn't. We all woke up basically naked, with a hangover from hell and vomit everywhere in the bathroom.

It took a while to remember what happened the night before, but we eventually put things together. I still have a scar on my wrist from her catching my sleeve on fire and ended up with the nickname bush man, but all of that is a story for another day.

How's the new job? School therapist?

Yes and it's great! How's everything going with you?

Everything's great. Can't wait to see you again.

You too.

Just like I'm not going to push for us all to get back together, I'm not going to push her to see me again, either. I know another reason she left was to put distance between all of us. She loves us and wanted to do what she thought was best. She thought she was an inconvenience and always putting us in danger, mainly because of her ex. While I don't agree, I understand. I'm sure she's not entirely comfortable inserting herself back into our lives, and that's okay. I'll keep texting her as I've always done the past six years and wait for her to be ready.

My assistant sent an itinerary for this week. I look it over and sigh at how packed it is. I just have to get through this week, so I can get back to Amelia.

CHAPTER SIXTEEN

AMELIA

It's Friday and Bash is finally back. He'll be in his office when I get there, and I couldn't be more excited. It was such a long week without seeing him. I missed him.

So, I'm nervous about today since I'm going to be seeing him again, but I'm also nervous because of the phone call I received thirty minutes ago.

I was offered the job at a school I applied for and interviewed for over the summer. They had filled the position, but the teacher just quit. I would start the first week of November and I have to give my answer to them by next Monday, so I have a little over a week to think about it.

I've spent the past thirty minutes getting ready and thinking about every pro and con about taking the job. It's what I wanted... right? I love teaching and it's something I'm passionate about. It's a great school in a good district. I feel like this should be a no brainer, and I should've immediately said yes, but I didn't.

With traffic, the school is about forty-five minutes away from Sierra's place. I don't have a car, so I would have to buy one and drive in this crazy New York traffic, or I would have to get an apartment closer. I haven't had a chance to look up how much it would be in that area, but I think I would be able to afford it. The salary for being a teacher is decent in that district, and I know I've only been here a couple months, but I've been able to save up a ton of money thanks to Sierra insisting I not pay for rent and save it to get back on my feet.

Even with the decent salary, it's not as much as I currently get paid. I don't love my current job, but I like it enough. It's fun working with Sierra, and I enjoy being able to see Bash whenever I want, even though we keep it as professional as possible while working.

I shake my head and finish getting ready for work. I know Sierra's waiting for me. I'm going to have to think more about this over the weekend and do some research. I don't think I'm going to tell her or Bash about it until I'm close to making my decision. I don't want either of them to influence what I choose to do.

When we make it to work, I immediately get a text from Bash asking me to come to his office. I tell Sierra and, of course, she literally pushes me his way and makes a joke about how she'll make sure no one interrupts us. I roll my eyes at her and enter after knocking.

When I close the door behind me, Bash looks up from his desk and his eyes darken. Butterflies form in my stomach under his gaze. Of course I made sure to put on the tightest, but professional outfit that I own. Yeah, I'm crossing the professional line that I drew. At least I can admit it.

He gets up, rounds his desk, and stands in front of me in less than two seconds. My back is flat against the door as he towers over me with a hand above my head.

"I missed you," he whispers in my ear.

I close my eyes and take a deep breath. Geez, I want to climb this man like a tree right now.

"I missed you too," I say on the breath out.

He stares me in the eyes and smirks. Ugh, he knows what he's doing to me. It's payback for wearing this outfit. I know it.

"I thought you said you wanted to keep things professional," he says.

"I do," I reply with a shaky breath.

"Then why are you wearing this?" He rubs his hand down the side of my body.

I tense at his touch because I want nothing more than to pull him to me right now and kiss him.

"It's professional, right?" I tease.

"It is... but I'm sorry. If you didn't want me to fuck you in my office, then you should've chosen something else," he says before slamming his mouth to mine.

This time I moan... loudly...

His hands are everywhere on my body and mine on his. I can't stop touching him everywhere and he feels the same. We haven't slept together since the one time on vacation. I enjoyed getting to know him better, but my body craves his and at this moment, I don't care if we're in the office and someone could walk in at any moment.

The lock clicks behind me. Clearly, he has the same agenda. I continue to kiss him and rub my hands through his hair. He grabs the back of my thighs and lifts me up as I wrap my legs around his waist.

Walking us over to his desk, he places my butt down on the edge and without breaking the kiss, he swipes his arm across the desk, sending the contents to the floor. Surprisingly, it's not as loud as I would expect with the force he pushed them off.

He pushes me further back on the desk, kissing down my neck and forcing me to lie on my back as he unbuttons my blouse. It lays open with my lacy white bra showing. He groans as he traces the lace on the bra and then drags his fingers down my stomach to my skirt. He unzips the side and takes it off in one pull, leaving my matching white panties on.

"So. Fucking. Beautiful," he says, looking at me with heavy eyes.

I try to sit up to unbutton his shirt, but he pushes me back down, holding me against the desk with his body weight.

"Not yet. Let me enjoy you for a bit," he says while pulling my underwear down and tossing it to join my skirt.

Normally, I would be cringing at my underwear sitting on the dirty floor, but I'm so turned on right now that I don't care. That thought turns nonexistent as he parts my legs, and his mouth finds its way between them.

I grab his hair and hold him against me as I shamelessly grind against his face. He's wasting no time, and I'm ready to explode. His moaning while he's licking and sucking sends me over the edge into the best orgasm I've ever had in my life.

He doesn't give me a chance to recover before he drags me off the desk and spins me around, pushing me down against it. My bra and half taken off blouse are still on with my high heels, while he's fully clothed.

His arm lies across my back, keeping my breasts and face pressed against the desk while I hear his belt unbuckle and pants unzip. He removes his arm for a few seconds to open his desk drawer and pull something out. I don't dare move as I hear the telltale rip of a condom wrapper.

He pushes down on me again while grabbing my hair gently, but firmly. He leans forward and kisses up my neck, reaching my ear.

"I've wanted to lean you over this desk and fuck you since the first day you walked into my office," he whispers in my ear as I shiver in anticipation.

He kicks my feet to spread my legs further apart and positions me higher on the desk, as he wastes no time slamming into me from behind. I let out the loudest moan, not caring that anyone standing outside this office can hear me.

"Mr. Hale..." I breathe out.

He moans as he slams into me over and over. "Yes baby. Let everyone hear that you're mine."

I can't help it. I can't keep quiet as he continues to quicken his pace and fucks me unapologetically hard. This is the most uncomfortable position with the desk digging into my stomach, but I don't care. I feel the heat rising in my core again as I come even harder than the first time.

He almost immediately follows behind me. "Fuck! Amelia..."

I love hearing my name on his lips as he comes undone. After taking a moment to catch our breaths, he slowly pulls out, and I watch him tie off the condom, tossing it in the wastebin by his desk.

I quickly grab my underwear and skirt from the floor, pulling them both back on while he zips up his pants and straightens his shirt. I'm not sure what to do or say at this moment, so I take my time buttoning my blouse, keeping my head down. Now that the post orgasm bliss has worn off, I feel... embarrassed. I don't know why I am, but I am.

Bash stands in front of me and takes over, buttoning my blouse. I don't look him in the eye, I can't.

After he's finished, he lifts my chin with his fingers and kisses me gently. "That was amazing, Amelia."

I can feel myself blushing. That was amazing. I've never done anything like that before and it felt good. Really good.

"It was," I say softly.

He kisses me again. It starts gentle but quickly turns into a more passionate kiss as I grab the back of his neck. My body is acting like he didn't just give me two orgasms, fucking me over his desk.

I bite his bottom lip, and he groans, pulling back. "We should stop here if you don't want me to take you back to my place and fuck you in every position possible for the rest of the day."

I smile and shake my head. That sounds amazing, but I know he has a busy schedule today, considering he's been out of the office for the past week. I can't be the reason he slacks on the job.

"That sounds fantastic, but we both know we have work to do. Maybe I can take a rain check for that next weekend?" I ask, hoping he'll say yes.

"Next weekend? Why not this weekend?" he asks, looking disappointed.

"I have plans this weekend, but next weekend is wide open so we can celebrate your birthday," I respond.

"Mmm. Then next weekend it is. You'll come home with me from work Friday, and we'll come back to the office together Monday," he says with a grin.

"While that sounds amazing, won't everyone know?" I ask concerned about what would happen if people found out we're together.

He shrugs. "Probably, but who cares? If anyone says anything to you, then send them to me."

I smile and kiss him. I meant for it to be a quick kiss, but he pulls me back in, not letting me go.

"Are you sure I can't convince you to skip work today?" he pleads.

"Sierra would kill me. Speaking of, I better get back to work," I say, pushing him away and walking toward the door.

"Amelia," he stops me before I open it.

"Yeah?" I turn back around to face him.

"I... I missed you. We'll talk later?" he asks and scratches the back of his head. He looks nervous again.

I nod before unlocking the door and leaving his office. I head directly to my desk and sit, thinking about what just happened. Oh my God. I just had sex with my boss in his office. The hottest sex I've ever had in my life. It was rough, hot, passionate, and perfect. I can't believe I just did that.

Closing my eyes, I try to clear my head. Sierra is going to come out of her office soon and demand to know what happened. I need to get myself together, so I can tell her the basics and not get flustered. I don't want to make a big deal about it, but I know I can't keep this from her. I smile as I try to concentrate on the new emails I received this morning.

CHAPTER SEVENTEEN

BASH

I can't believe I just fucked Amelia on my desk. I groan as I'm instantly hard thinking about it again. When I asked her to come into my office this morning, I just wanted to see her and tell her I missed her. The moment she walked in and I saw the tight blouse and skirt she was wearing, I lost it. I literally had no control. I had to have her right then.

Thankfully, she didn't object. I didn't mean to be so rough with her when I fucked her against my desk. I couldn't help myself. She didn't seem to mind it. In fact, she seemed to enjoy it. Fuck. My dick stirs in my pants again. She's not as delicate as she seems to be. I wonder what else she's willing to do in bed. I intend to find out next weekend as I'm not going to let her leave my bed.

I shake my head, trying to get these thoughts out of it. I really have a lot of work to do today as I've been out of the office all week. I hate coming back to work on a Friday. While I try to respond to some emails, a text comes through on my phone.

Ben

> Since Everly's back in town lets get to-
> gether. I checked everyone's schedule
> and we're all free tomorrow night. My
> place 6 pm.

I look at my calendar and see it's clear. I actually don't have anything going on all weekend, which is why I was disappointed when she said she was busy this weekend. I wonder what her plans are.

I watch my phone for a minute to see if any other texts come through, but they don't. Ben convinced us all to give him access to our schedules forever ago. I didn't really mind, and I guess he still has it. I have a feeling even if I took him off it, he would still find a way to access it. We're waiting for James' response. So, if Ben says that everyone's schedule is clear, then he doesn't have plans. It's a matter of if he wants to get all of us together again and face Jake.

James' response finally comes.

James

I'll be there.

I have to say that I'm surprised. I thought he might make up an excuse for why he can't come, but I can also see that he wouldn't want Everly to be there without him while Jake is there. This is going to be an interesting night.

I arrive at Ben's apartment building at the same time Jake does. Convenient, since I wanted to talk with him before we go in.

"Hey," I say to Jake as the doorman opens the door for us.

"Hey," Jake responds, looking nervous.

Everyone knows us, so we're immediately brought to the elevator and buzzed up to Ben's floor. James lives on the floor above him.

As we ride the elevator, I try to make the conversation quick. "Everything going to be okay tonight?"

He knows what I'm asking. "On my end it is."

I place my arm around his shoulder and squeeze as we step off the elevator. I pull him back to indicate I want to talk a little longer before we head inside.

I face him toward me. "I've got your back, you know. I always do, but I'm asking you to not start anything."

He chuckles. "Yeah, I know. Thanks bro. I promise everything's good on my end."

I nod and knock on the door. Ben opens it and as I step in, I find James on the left side of the couch with a beer. He looks uptight and serious like he usually does, but his grown out dirty blonde hair makes him seem more approachable. Unless you're Jake.

I make my way to him first and pat him on the shoulder, sitting right beside him. His dark green eyes are focused on my brother, and he's glaring at him with his hand gripped on the beer a little too tight.

I try to lighten the mood. "If looks could kill, Jake would be dead."

James smirks. "If only."

I shake my head. "You gotta let it go man, it's not good for you and if you want Everly back... he's one of her best friends too, so he's not going anywhere."

James lets out a low growl and seems lost in his thoughts until Jake sits in the chair next to the couch on his side. I give Jake a warning look, knowing he purposefully sat there to piss off James.

"Hey James, good to see you," Jake says in a friendly tone.

While I think he really is trying, I know that's going to set James off. Thankfully, James just doesn't respond. I let out the breath I was holding while seeing how that played out. James stands and heads to the other room. I assume he's going to the bathroom to take a moment before Everly gets here. Jake and I stay seated while Ben joins us, sitting in the other chair.

Ben looks over at me and asks, "So how long do you think it'll be before these two get into it?"

Jake laughs and I chuckle, opening a beer of my own. "I give it five minutes after Everly's here."

"Hey, it's not going to be started by me," Jake says, holding his hands up.

We both know he's right. James will look for every and any opportunity to have it out with Jake. James is one of my best friends and like my brother, but I wasn't lying to Jake when I said I'll have his back no matter what. Even if Jake started it, I've got his back. He's my brother, I have to, and I'll deal with him later.

"Jake, that's your seat. Stay there. You know James is going to want to put her the furthest from you. Just let him," I say, hoping he'll agree.

Jake nods. "Of course. I know they're working on their relationship. I'm not going to fuck it up."

I want to say that I'm surprised Jake is being so agreeable to everything, but I'm not. I'm not entirely sure if he's over her completely, but I am positive that he loves her enough to want her happy. He knows that James will make her happy, and they belong together. We all see it. He's not going to mess with her happiness.

Another knock on the door indicates that Everly has arrived. Ben opens the door, and Jake is immediately there, already talking and laughing with her. He grabs her into a hug, lifts her, and spins her around. I shake my head and smile because that's Jake.

James walks toward Everly and gives her a hug that lasts a lot longer than it needs to.

"Hey," Everly says to him, looking at him like she's already fallen in love with him again.

"Hey," James says back, equally looking like a lovesick dog.

Usually, that would make me sick and wanting to look away, but it just makes me think of Amelia. When she was leaving my office yesterday after our... encounter, I had the urge to tell her I love her. I stopped myself because it scared me. It got me thinking, do I love her? We haven't been together that long. Is it possible to love someone in such a short amount of time? Would it have scared her away if I had told her?

My attention is brought back to the moment as I watch them head over to sit, so I scoot to where James was sitting, which will place me closer to Jake. Sure enough, James places himself beside me in the middle, and Everly next to him, the furthest possible from Jake, while still keeping her sitting by him.

The next hour is filled with laughter and reminiscing about the old days. I'm pleasantly surprised that Jake and James haven't had an issue yet. James has been giving Jake looks, but he hasn't said anything, which is a little awkward since we're all talking, and they aren't. Well, I'd say there were one or two comments James threw out at Jake, but thankfully Jake laughed them off. It really feels like no time has passed between us, other than we're clearly older.

Everly hasn't changed much, but she's definitely become a beautiful woman. When she first came to live with the Crawfords that summer, she was tiny and thin. Now she is toned and looks great. It must be from all the training she does with Declan, her security guard. I'm glad to see that she has continued with that and wants to keep herself safe. I have a feeling that she could win in a fight against me, even though I work out almost every morning and spar with Jake often. Though, it has been a bit since we did that.

She has long brown hair, but it has a hint of red in it and loose curls. Her eyes are hazel while her skin is pale. She has always been pale, even when she spends a little time outside. Though it doesn't look like she has spent much time in the sun at all recently.

I watch James and Everly as they seem to be in their own little world. Ben and Jake are talking about the games we used to play when we were younger. Ben mentions never have I ever, that we should play, and I can't help but smile. That's a good one.

"Never have I ever, that's been a while," I say in agreement.

"Last time we played, we went skinny dipping in the lake and then got drunk. Can we remember what we said? I wonder if we can say never have I ever still to some of them," Ben says.

"Oh, that's fun. Good idea Ben. We'll take a drink if we have done it," Everly says while opening a second beer.

James picks up his beer and says, "I remember one of mine, and it still holds true. Never have I ever kissed a boy."

Everly drinks her beer, and we all look around at each other. None of the rest of us takes a sip.

"You still haven't Jake? I'm surprised," Ben teases.

Jake shrugs his shoulders. "What can I say? I like women too much."

Everly clears her throat and says, "Well, I remember that one came right after mine, which was never have I ever kissed a girl."

We all wait for her response to see if it still holds true. She shrugs her shoulders and takes a drink. We all roar and hoot as Jake yells out he needs the details.

Everly laughs. "I was completely drunk with my friends, and I kissed a couple of them. No big deal, sorry there's nothing juicy to tell."

Even so, that's pretty hot. I can tell everyone else is thinking the same, and it takes a moment for us all to settle down.

I clear my throat. "One of mine was never have I ever failed a class. That still holds true."

Jake, Ben, and Everly take a swig of their beers. We knew Jake and Ben had because of last time, but this is new for Everly. I'm curious which class she failed, but that's a time in her life that's probably best left to the past.

I look at Ben and Jake to see if they remember theirs, but they both say they don't. We're all lost in thought, trying to think back to seven years ago.

Apparently, Everly remembers. "Ben, yours was that you never peed in the shower. Please tell me that doesn't still hold true."

Ben laughs. "Sorry Everly, that's still true. I just can't bring myself to do it."

The rest of us take another swig of our beers as we laugh. Ben has a weird thing about showers and bathrooms in general, so that's not surprising. We all stare at Jake as if it'll make one of us remember his. The look on his face makes me know that he does remember and just doesn't want to say it. It took a moment, but I now remember what it was. Shit. Yeah, Jake's doing his best not to start anything with James.

"Come on Jake, I can tell you remember. What was it? Clearly it doesn't still hold true if you don't want to say it," Ben says, trying to get it out of him.

I look over at Ben and harden my stare. Ben obviously doesn't remember what it was, or he wouldn't be pushing Jake to say it.

Jake shrugs his shoulders. "Nah, I don't remember. I was pretty drunk that night."

Looking around the room, I can tell that no one is going to back down on this. I appreciate Jake trying to be good, but at this point, it'll be easier to get it over with. Plus, James' face tells me he knows exactly what it was.

"Come on, Jake, what was it?" I step in, trying to give him a look that it's okay.

Jake gives me a pleading look back to help him out of this, but I shake my head and try to give him a look to remind him I'm on his side.

I watch James remove his arm from behind Everly's shoulders and stiffen beside her. He aggressively says, "Yeah, come on, Jake. Tell us what it was. I know you'll take a swig for this one."

Jake looks at Everly apologetically before revealing, "Alright, if you insist, James. Mine was never have I ever had sex with Everly. Clearly that doesn't still stand."

Jake takes a sip of his beer while James leans back and takes an equally long sip of his beer. They both eye each other while they do so. We're all quiet as we watch the tension grow, wondering if this is going to be the moment James snaps.

I sit forward, ready to defend my brother if needed, but clear my throat and change the topic. "Well, that was fun. So, what are you guys doing for Halloween this year? It's my parents' turn for the annual Halloween party, so it'll be at their house this year. Bring a date, I'll be bringing my girlfriend. You all in?"

Everly sits forward before excitedly saying, "Yes! I love a good Halloween party. I'll be there, but first I need details about this girlfriend!"

Leaning back, I smile as I think about Amelia. I can't wait for them to meet her.

"We've only been dating for a couple of months, but she's amazing and beautiful," I say.

"Okay, more details, please. What's her name and where did you meet?" Everly asks while leaning over James to get a better look at me.

"Her name's Amelia and we met over the summer while I was on our work vacation at the resort. Everything's still new, but I really like her."

"I can't wait to meet her," she says.

Ben interrupts, changing the subject back. "I'm in for the party."

"Well, it's my parents too, so I have no choice but to be there," Jake says.

"I'll be there," James says while continuing to stare at Everly.

"Alright, it sounds like we have our next group night planned," I say while the smile still hasn't faded from my face.

Shortly after, James and Everly leave. Jake and I help Ben pick up for a bit before heading out together. I thank Ben for hosting tonight and tell him it was good seeing him again.

"You did good, Jake," I say, putting my arm around his shoulder as we walk onto the elevator.

"Yeah," he says, looking like he's defeated.

"What?" I ask, turning him to face me.

"It's nothing," he says while putting on his fake smile.

You'd think he'd realize that I know him better than that. His fake smiles will never trick me.

"What's going on?" I ask him seriously.

"Seriously, it's nothing. I'm glad they're happy together. You can see it, you know, their love. And I can tell how much you're in love with Amelia. It's great. I'm just..." he trails off.

"Jealous?" I ask.

He shrugs. "Nah, not really jealous. I don't know what I'm feeling."

Yeah, I get what he means. Well, I've never been in his situation before. He fell in love, and she didn't love him back. Now he sees all his friends happy and in love and he wants that too. It's nothing for him to be ashamed of. The man is a freaking teddy bear inside. He just wants to be loved and sometimes I wonder if it has to do with our parents never showing their love for us. That's why I want him to know that I always have his back. That I'll always love him.

"Let's go grab a drink," I say as we exit the apartment building.

Chapter Eighteen

AMELIA

This week has been a fucking shit week. I take a deep breath in and let it out slowly, leaning my head back against my chair. Okay, I need to calm down. I really try to keep my cool and not curse, but I feel like after the week I've had, it's warranted. I'm going to let myself curse as much as I need to in order to feel better.

Not only was work horrible, but I feel like everything is just going wrong. To start the week off, my laptop died Monday morning, and it can't be fixed. I'm trying to save as much money as possible, but I had to order a new laptop using Sierra's computer. Why couldn't I use my phone to order one? Oh, that's because my phone broke when I got out of the car for work that very same day.

Sierra drove me to work, as usual, and when I stepped out of the car, my phone fell out of my pocket... at the same moment I was closing the car door. Needless to say, it was crushed and damaged beyond repair. So, I purchased a new laptop and a new phone on the same day.

Tuesday rolled around, and Bash got called away on another business trip. He won't be back until Friday afternoon. I don't feel like I should be this clingy to him already, but I am. I miss him and wish he was here when I have a bad day. He made me feel better after my horrible Monday, and that's mainly just because he was there and listened to me rant. He offered to pay for my new laptop and phone, but obviously I declined.

So, I guess Tuesday wasn't awful, but I was just in my feels. Wednesday was a shitty day. Literally shitty. When I was walking to get lunch for Sierra and myself, I got shit on by a fucking bird. I swear it aimed just for me. There were so many people around, but it chose me! The brownish white shit was all over my hair and jacket. Instead of grabbing our lunch, I walked back into Sierra's office to show her what the offending bird did to me. She laughed her ass off the whole way to the bathroom and as she tried to help me wash it out of my hair.

She ended up sending someone else to grab our lunch and then she continued to enjoy her good laugh about my unfortunate situation. Thirty minutes after eating, I was in the bathroom with an upset stomach. Whatever I ate didn't agree with me, and I was in there four more times before heading home. If that wasn't bad enough, the last time I used the bathroom at work, the toilet clogged. Shit was literally rising and there was nothing I could do about it. I ran and got the maintenance guy,

Joe, and he happily fixed the situation. I was embarrassed as fuck and wanted to die.

When Thursday hit, I figured that it surely couldn't be much worse than the first half of the week. I maniacally laugh just thinking about that. I'm so stupid. Clearly, I did something the past few weeks to deserve the bad luck I've had this week.

My stomach still wasn't fully healed, so I felt off the whole day. When we got to work, it started pouring, and I stepped in a giant puddle, soaking my shoes and socks. Sierra somehow missed the whole thing, and she was basically dry when we entered the building while I looked like a drowned rat. I'm confused, it's like every rain drop purposely avoided her and said, "Oh there's Amelia, let's get her!" Whatever, fine.

I was soaked and kept having to take off my socks and shoes when I was at my desk trying to get them to dry faster. One time Sierra called me into her office, and I forgot she had an important client in there, so I didn't put my shoes back on. We all just stared at each other, and I quietly backed out without saying a word and closed the door. I put on my shoes and went back in like nothing happened. Yeah, the client didn't act like nothing happened. He just looked at me like I was a freak. Fine, I probably am.

After that, I just became an emotional wreck and broke down in the bathroom. I ended up calling Bash, crying, while sitting on the disgusting bathroom floor. I care more about it now, but in that moment, I was so worked up I didn't even care. Bash did his best to make me feel better, and ultimately, he did. He even offered to come back from his trip early, but I refused to let him. I could survive one more day without him.

I almost didn't survive another day without him. This morning when I went to get us some coffee, I was almost hit by a car. I was crossing the crosswalk when I was supposed to, but he didn't get the memo he needed to stop. A nice man was able to pull me out of the way at the last second, but I thought I was literally going to die. I felt so nauseous and threw up a moment later. I've never been that worked up before, but I suppose after the week I've had and almost dying, it was only a natural response for my body to produce.

When I made it back with the coffee, there was a client waiting at my desk. I felt bad not being able to bring Sierra her coffee before her meeting, which lasted another thirty minutes. Anyway, this man insisted that he had a meeting at nine with Sierra, when his meeting wasn't until eleven. I had to hold my tongue, be nice to him, and apologize for the mistake, even though I knew there was no mistake. Especially since I opened the email exchange between us, and he clearly wrote eleven. When I tried to bring this fact up, he started accusing me of faking the email, being a liar, and calling me nasty names.

Thankfully, Sierra came out shortly after, and he acted like he was the nicest person alive to her. She squeezed him in for the meeting, and I sat at my desk fuming. When he came out of her office, his demeanor changed again as he continued to berate me for my apparent mistake and told me how he would be emailing Bash personally to get me fired. Ricky, a security guard, overheard the exchange and escorted him out. I had to fill Sierra in on what he said to me, and she promised they wouldn't be doing business with him in the future.

So, I made it through the workday without any more crazy incidents, but now I'm sitting at my desk literally pulling at my hair, thinking about that asshole and everything he said to me.

I catch sight of Bash coming toward me. He stands in front of my desk, smiling down at me. I let out a breath and smile back. It's so fucking good to see him.

"I've missed you," he says, leaning toward me, kissing me on the forehead.

"I've missed you too."

"What are you in the mood for, babe?" he asks with his cocky smile.

"I'm in the mood for tying my hair to the ceiling fan and going for a fucking spin." I swirl my finger in the air, emphasizing the spin.

"... I meant for dinner..." he whispers, looking at me questionably.

"Oh, pizza sounds good."

"You sure? Sounds like you could use a margarita or something."

"Why would you say that?" I ask, but obviously I know the answer. He's not wrong.

He laughs, and it makes me feel ten times better. It amazes me how a simple laugh from Bash can make my shitty week feel so distant. I pack my things quickly and grab the duffle bag I stashed in Sierra's office. I'm going home with Bash tonight, and I hope he's not expecting to sleep because I plan to keep him up all night.

After ordering pizza and getting settled in Bash's apartment, we get comfortable on the couch and search for a movie to watch. While I wanted to jump his bones the moment we stepped foot inside the door, he insisted we eat dinner first and spend some time together. Dang him for being a gentleman.

As we're searching through Netflix, Bash stops on a Halloween movie and looks over at me.

"I forgot to ask you something. I kind of told my friends that I'll be bringing my girlfriend to my parents' Halloween party this year..." he trails off.

I lift my eyebrow at him. "Kind of?"

He laughs. "I told them I'm bringing you, and they are really excited to meet you. Will you come with me?"

I think about it for a moment. He wants me to attend his parents' Halloween party? So not only am I going to be meeting his parents, but also his friends? It's not that I don't want to, but it sounds really overwhelming. If Bash is as rich as he is, his parents must be richer. I'm sure all of his friends are in the same filthy rich category and I'm... me. I don't live on my own, and

I don't have a car. I don't really have anything to my name. I'm just an assistant, which I only got the job because of my best friend.

Bash places his hand on mine. "Hey, talk to me. Do you already have plans?"

I shake my head. "No, I don't. It's just... Are you sure you want me to meet your parents and friends?"

He grins. "Is that what you're worried about? Of course I want you to meet them. I've been talking about you since you started at my company. Everyone wants to meet you."

"What if they don't like me? I have a feeling I won't... fit in," I say.

"My brother met you and he likes you," he states seriously.

"I have a feeling your brother likes every girl he interacts with."

Bash lets out a deep laugh. "You're not far off, but no, not every girl. He's a good judge of character, so if he says you're alright, then I guess you're good for me."

This time I laugh. "Okay, good to know. I better not get on Jake's bad side, or you'll break up with me."

"So, will you come?" he asks again, looking unsure of what the answer will be.

"Yeah, okay. It sounds fun. Should I dress as something specific?"

"I'll let you know. My buddy James texted he's going to send us characters to dress as. He's trying to win back his ex..." he states, trailing off at the end.

He picks up his phone and begins typing out a message. "Sorry, this reminded me I forgot to text someone this week."

He continues typing his message out when the pizza arrives at the door. I'm about to get up to get it, but he jumps up first and places his phone on the couch. I watch him walk toward the front door and feel his phone vibrate on the couch next to me.

I'm not in the habit of reading other people's texts, but his phone is right there with his text thread still open. I would've just looked away, but the "love you" catches my attention. Quickly scanning the texts, I find the name on the text thread is Everly.

> It was great seeing you the other night. You looked beautiful and I've missed you. I can't wait for our next night together.

Everly

> Thank you handsome. See you soon, love you!

I feel sick to my stomach but quickly toss the phone back on the couch when I hear Bash returning. My mind is racing with everything and nothing at the same time.

He places the pizza on the coffee table in front of me and says, "I'm going to hit the bathroom real fast. Help yourself."

All I can do is nod as he walks out of the room. I pick up his phone to scan the messages again to see if I imagined them. I did not. In fact, as I continue to scroll back, there are more and more messages that go on for weeks, even months, just like that one.

The tears prick at my eyes, but I can't let them fall yet. Bash will only be gone for another moment, so I need to decide what I want to do. Should I stay and bring this up to him? Maybe it's not what it seems. Or maybe he's had a girlfriend all this time, and he's been cheating on her with me. Oh my God, am I the other woman in this situation? Is that where he's been going on his business trips? He's been visiting her? Was he screwing her all week while I was having a shitty week? What the fuck is with this week?

I've made my decision. I need to get out of here. I feel bad that I'm ruining the birthday celebration we planned, but I'm overwhelmed with emotions. It's best if I leave before he comes back. Thankfully, I didn't unpack my duffle, and it's still by the front door. I grab my duffle and shoes, not bothering to put them on, and leave.

CHAPTER NINETEEN

BASH

When I come back from the bathroom, I find the couch empty. I scan the room, but don't see Amelia anywhere.

"Amelia?" I call out, listening for any signs of her.

I'm about to scour the apartment, but I notice her shoes and duffle bag missing from the entrance. She left? I quickly search for my phone to find it on the couch where we were sitting. I dial her number, but it goes straight to voicemail. Crap. I dial Wells next.

"What's up?" he answers.

"Did Amelia leave?" I ask, knowing that he gets notifications every time someone enters or leaves my floor.

"Yes," he states calmly.

"And?" I ask, wanting him to tell me everything, like he knows what's going on.

"And what? She left about two minutes ago. I'll pull up the footage."

"I'll come over," I say, already heading out my door and down the hall to his apartment.

I own the whole floor. There's my apartment, Wells' apartment, and another one that sits empty on this floor. There's also a security room, but I don't often have security sitting and watching. It's there whenever there is a threat that needs to be monitored.

He already has his door open for me to enter when I get there. We both walk to his setup with three monitors. We waste no time pulling up the hallway feed and watch Amelia leave my apartment with her duffle over her shoulder and barefoot as she carries her shoes out. Why was she in so much of a hurry that she couldn't take the time to put on her shoes?

"Go to my living room cameras. I want to see what she was doing when I was in the bathroom," I state calmly.

I may sound calm, but I'm anything but. I feel sick knowing that something is wrong, and I don't know what. I'm also pissed that her phone is turned off.

We watch the camera in the living room starting from when I was talking to her about Halloween and until I got up to get the pizza. When I leave, I notice her picking up my phone and looking at it for only a moment before I get back. When I leave again, she picks it up again and starts scrolling through it. She freezes like she's debating something and then bolts off the couch, grabs her stuff, and leaves.

What the fuck did she see on my phone that warranted that reaction? Why was she looking at my phone in the first place? I pull it out and there's nothing on my screen. I pull up my texts and don't see anything unusual.

"It looks like she didn't like something she saw on your phone," Wells states.

"Yeah, I know. I can't figure out what though," I say.

"Let me see it."

I give it over to him and he looks through it. He has access to all my messages and information anyway, so I don't care if he looks at it. He knows everything about my life. It's not private. It's the only way to ensure that he keeps me safe.

"Well, I think I found what scared her off," he says, handing the phone back to me.

My messages with Everly are pulled up, and I read the message she sent back. Her message thread didn't show that it was unread, so he's right. Amelia must have read my messages to her. My heart stops as I read Everly's newest message and place myself in Amelia's shoes of not knowing what they mean.

"Shit. She thinks I'm cheating on her," I state as I race out the door.

"I'll drive," Wells says on my tail.

I'm not going to argue with him because there's no point. He'll insist on driving, especially knowing the emotional state I'm currently in. It's probably for the best. I can't believe I wasn't upfront with her about Everly and the type of texts that we share. I should have been clear with her from the beginning because even I know these look bad.

We pull up to Sierra's apartment after I try calling Amelia ten more times. They all go straight to voicemail. I fucked up.

I push the button to Sierra's apartment, and it goes unanswered. It's the same result when I try again. Come on, she has to be here. I call Sierra and thankfully she answers.

"Yes boss?"

"Are you home?" I ask, getting straight to it.

"Why?" she asks suspiciously.

"Because I'm outside your apartment asking to be let up," I state like it's a normal thing that I do on a Friday night.

"Is there something you need?"

"Yes, to be let up," I say, getting more frustrated.

"You'll have to be more specific than that. If it's work related, then I'm going to ask for you to get back with me on Monday," she states sweetly.

Fuck. Amelia is definitely there, and she already told Sierra. If I call, which is rare, Sierra will do whatever is needed, even on the weekend.

I sigh and lean against the wall. "Sierra, there's been a misunderstanding, and I just need to talk to Amelia for five minutes."

There's a long pause before she responds, "Amelia isn't here right now."

"You and I both know that's a lie."

She doesn't respond.

My voice becomes desperate. "Please Sierra. If you won't let me up, then just let me talk to her on the phone. Please."

She sighs. "I'm sorry Bash."

I close my eyes and keep my emotions in check. "Is there anything I can do to change your mind?"

There's another long pause, and I hear a door click closed. "It's not my place. Just... give her some time to think, okay? I told you she just got out of a bad relationship."

I cut her off before she can say anything else. "I know, but I don't want her thinking the wrong thing. What she thinks she saw isn't true. I would never hurt her like that. I really like her, Sierra."

"I know..." she whispers.

"Alright, I'll give her time. Can you just... tell her to call me when she's ready to talk?"

"I will."

"Thanks." I hang up the phone.

I stare at Wells, who is looking at me with pity. Fuck. Rarely does he look at me like that or get invested in my private life. He may know everything about me, but he's not emotionally attached. I don't need his pity.

"Ready?" he asks.

"Yeah," I say with my head hanging low as I enter the car and try to figure out how to fix this.

I'm drunk. I'm at the bar that I ran into Amelia, in hopes that maybe she needed a drink tonight too and would be here. Unfortunately, she wasn't. Wells has been trying to get me to leave for the past hour, but I'm not budging. I don't remember the last time I was this drunk. It's been a while.

Someone plops down noisily beside me, but I don't bother to look over. I'm sure they'll leave in the next thirty minutes or so, just like the last person. Though, unlike the last person, this one places their hand on my shoulder.

"Bash, let's go home," the familiar voice says.

I finally look over to find my brother staring down at me. He doesn't look like his normal self, and I don't think it's just because he's starting to spin. Ugh, why did I drink so much? I'm going to regret this in the morning, if not in two seconds.

"I think I'm going to just stay here and die. Thanks," I slur.

"Nah. How many times have you dragged my ass out of bars? It's time for me to return the favor."

I laugh, I think. It might have been more like a groan. I'm not sure.

"Come on. I've got you," he says, helping me off my chair.

I fall over into him, but he grips me tighter, and I'm pretty sure he's basically carrying me out the door. Before I know it, I'm in the car, lying down in the back seat. My head is on Jake's lap, and I feel pathetic.

I must have dozed because the next thing I know I'm being escorted into my apartment by Wells and Jake. He leads me to my bedroom, and I faceplant the bed. I should really change my clothes, brush my teeth, or even just move up on my bed so I don't fall off, but I don't do anything.

Jake pulls at my shirt and struggles to get it off. "Come on man. Help me out a little."

"Are you undressing me?" I groan.

"Yep. You'll thank me in the morning."

I manage to sit up, and he takes my shirt off and then the rest of my clothes, minus my boxers. I should be embarrassed or something, but I couldn't careless at the moment. Usually, I sleep in just my boxers or a pair of sweats, so this works for me.

Jake helps me into the center of the bed and instead of getting me under the comforter, he finds a blanket to throw over me.

"I'll be on the couch if you need something," he says, walking toward the door.

"You know I have a guest room," I mumble.

He chuckles. "Yeah, but the couch is closer when you need me to help you."

"Suit yourself," I say.

"Night big bro," he says, turning off the light.

"Jake?"

"Yeah?"

I pause for a moment before continuing. "I fucked up. I lost her. I really like her, and I screwed it up."

"I know. We'll talk in the morning. Get some sleep," he says, and everything goes black shortly after he leaves the room.

Chapter Twenty

AMELIA

Taking a deep breath, I look around the empty apartment and feel nauseous. I want to run away and never return. I want to go to a cabin in the middle of nowhere and never speak to anyone again. Would it be acceptable to just start over with a new identity and never return?

Sierra's hand rests on my shoulder as she gives it a little squeeze. "It's going to be okay, Amelia. One day at a time, remember?"

I nod and turn back toward the nice lady showing us the apartment. "This looks great. Can I get the information for it?"

Her smile beams back at me. "Of course! Let's go back to my office, and I can pull everything up."

An hour and a half later, my name is officially on the lease, and the apartment is mine to move into tomorrow. I honestly thought that it would take a couple weeks to be available, but it's completely ready for me like it's meant to be.

After leaving Bash's apartment Friday night, I took an Uber back to Sierra's place. I called her while waiting for it, then broke down in the back of the nice man's car. I turned my phone off right after we hung up. By the time I got to her apartment, she had a warm bath going for me and some wine. I drank the whole bottle.

I laid in bed all weekend and felt bad for myself, but Monday morning, I woke up with new determination. I decided I'd start living my life for myself and not relying on other people. Sierra has done so much for me, and I appreciate it, but it was time for me to move out and start my own life without a man. I emailed the school that offered me the position and accepted. I started looking at apartments near the school I'd be working at and found one within walking distance. If I didn't feel like walking one day or it was raining, I could get an Uber. I don't feel the need to get a car.

The apartment is cozy and perfect for me. It's a small studio apartment, with a bathroom and a kitchen. It has everything I need. I don't have family that comes to visit me, and I don't really have any friends. If I want to spend the night with Sierra, I'll just go to her place. It's about a forty-five-minute drive, but it's not bad. The only thing I don't like about it is that it's only about twenty or so minutes from Bash's apartment. I would've liked to be an hour away, but at least it's not right where he is, so most likely I won't be bumping into him anywhere. He's in the rich part of the city anyway.

My phone rings to find my new employer calling. I answer on the first ring.

"Hello?"

"Miss Hart?" the lady on the other end asks.

"This is her," I say, feeling stupid every time I respond like that.

"Good afternoon. I was calling to inform you that your position will actually be available starting Monday. I wanted to see if you'd be willing to start work a little earlier than planned," she says.

Excitedly, I answer, "Yes! I can be there Monday morning."

"Great. Thank you for working with us on this. I'll see you then," she states.

"Thank you. See you then," I respond, waiting for her to hang up the phone first.

My heart is racing with nerves as I finish packing the few personal belongings I have in boxes and make a list of needs for the apartment. I don't have anything, including a couch. Sierra said she'll take me shopping for some items tomorrow. She took a few days off work to help me with apartment hunting, and since we found one quickly, she has time to help me get settled in.

I don't have a ton of money to furnish the place, but if I'm not purchasing a car, I can get some decent items. I plan to get a couch for the living room, a bed, an end table, kitchen items, and anything else that's necessary. Everything else can wait. Sierra wasn't pleased when I said I wanted to shop at the dollar tree for all my kitchen and bathroom items, but she's not going to push it. Right now, I don't need to spend a lot on dishes. I can get everything there I need for the price of an expensive plate and bowl set. Honestly, I like their plates and stuff there. They work just the same.

I'm used to not spending money and shopping cheaply. Thrift stores are my best friends. I thought about getting my furniture there, but that's where Sierra drew the line. She told me she would buy my furniture for me if I insisted on that route, so I'm not. My anxiety really likes having a large cushion in savings, just in case.

A message lights up on my phone. My heart stops beating when I see the message is from Bash, again.

Bash

I heard you won't be returning to work. Can we please talk?

My throat feels tight as I fight back the tears again. I should block him. I should just do it, but I can't find it in me to. I don't know if it's because I know I should hear him out and find closure to this situation, or if it's just because I like torturing myself. Either way, I slide the phone back in my pocket and ignore it like the other twenty texts he has sent me.

I know Bash came after me that Friday night and wanted to talk, but I couldn't. I was too emotional, and I honestly didn't want to hear what he had to say. He's cheating on me, or technically her, whatever. I can't be with another cheater, even if it's looking like all guys are like that. I guess I'm destined to be alone forever.

As I lay on my bed, more memories of my ex pop into my thoughts, even though I try to will them away.

As I read the private messages on Jay's social media account, I feel sick. So sick. Tears instantly fall, and I'm holding back the vomit that wants to make an appearance. A few messages stand out the most to show me exactly what this is.

Babe your new pic looks hot!

I miss you too. We'll find time to get together soon.

I'm planning on breaking up with the bitch soon.

Beautiful. You and your perfect body are beautiful. I'll come visit again soon.

I have to stop reading before I throw his laptop against the wall and break it. What am I supposed to do with this? I know Jay and I have our issues, but I didn't think he'd cheat on me. I also didn't think he wanted to break up. How could he do this to me? I've done so much for him!

Jay walks out of the bathroom at this time and sees my face. He rolls his eyes and asks, "What's wrong now?"

I maniacally laugh. "Really? What's wrong now? Are you cheating on me Jay?"

My voice breaks on the last part.

He looks angry. "No, why would you think that?"

I turn his laptop around and show him the messages that are up on his screen. His eyes narrow as he looks at me accusingly.

"You're looking through my messages?" he asks, snatching the laptop and closing the screen.

"I wasn't, but it popped up."

"What the fuck were you doing on my computer anyway? It's mine. You aren't allowed to use it," he says angrily.

Yeah, now I can see why he's so possessive of his phone and laptop. He didn't want me to catch him cheating. How did I not suspect something before? I thought he was just a private person, and that was normal in relationships.

"I was just trying to order some pizza while my phone charges in the other room," I state, defending myself, even though I know I shouldn't be.

"Well don't touch my shit. Why are you ordering pizza when your ass is home and should be making a meal? You waste too much money all the time. No wonder you can't afford to help with rent," he spits.

Ouch. Now I'm angry and begin yelling. "You're joking, right? I do so fucking much around here and you insisted on paying for the rent. I've offered to help, but you said no."

He gets up in my face, and the spark of terror appears through my body like lightning. "Excuse me, bitch? I pay rent because I know you just throw your money away, and I wanted to take care of you. That's what men do, right? Take care of their women? Especially when they don't have a job."

I want to close my eyes and crawl into my own skin, but I'm afraid to close them for even half a second around him. I don't know what he'll do now that he's so worked up. He hasn't hit me in a few years, but he's been increasingly getting angrier and angrier lately. I know better than to push him, but for some reason, I couldn't help myself. Regardless, I know that look on his face, and that's one where my head might be slammed into the wall if I don't tread carefully.

I take a deep breath and let it out, whispering, "I'm sorry. I didn't mean to look at your messages."

He doesn't relax, which scares me. "What did you read?"

I shake my head, not wanting to answer him, or even think about it.

I didn't even realize I was taking steps back as he took steps forward. I'm backed up against the wall with the door across the room. My heart pounds even harder.

"I asked what you read!" he yells in my face.

I answer in a small voice. "You were calling her beautiful and said you wanted to meet up."

He laughs and backs up a little. "So, you think that means I'm cheating on you? She's just a friend."

I know better, I do, but I can't help myself. "You called her beautiful. You never call me beautiful."

He stalks forward again. "Maybe if you took better care of yourself, you'd be beautiful."

The tears burn at the back of my eyes, and the anger rises once again. He's such a jerk. What is wrong with me? Why have I been with him this whole time? He's clearly cheating on me and he's lying. I need to leave.

I take a step to the side, and he grabs my arm. "Where do you think you're going?"

"I'm leaving," I respond.

"I didn't say we were done with this conversation," he pushes me back against the wall.

I don't want to push him too much, but I can't stay here anymore either.

"I think you're better off with her. I'll just take a few of my things and leave," I state as calmly as I can.

Now the anger in his face and voice comes back. "You're not leaving. You leave, then you leave all your shit. It's mine. I pay for this place. Everything in it is mine."

I take a quick breath in. "You can't do that. I'll call the police if I need to."

He laughs again. "Do it. Call them. I'll show them how the lease is in my name, how I pay for it every month, and I'll find a way to prove that everything here is mine as well. Your precious books are mine. You'll never get them back."

At this point, I don't care. I need to get out of here before this escalates more, and I'll figure the rest out later. I use my other hand to loosen his grip on me, but he just grabs me harder. Stepping to the side, my back isn't against the wall anymore, and I try to pull my arm away. He gets angry and pulls me closer to him.

"Please, just let me go. We'll talk about this later when we've calmed down," I plead with him.

"I told you, you're not leaving me," he says.

I shake my head. "Please. I just want to take a few minutes to calm down. Then we'll talk, I promise."

I have no intention of talking to him or working this out. We've been in this same moment too many times to count, but this time is different. I really have nothing more to lose. I don't have a job anymore, I don't have friends here, and I don't have him. I've already lost him to someone else. I need to get the courage to finally leave.

"Where are you going to go? Huh bitch? There's no one for you to run to. Your parents don't want you and you don't have any friends. Your only friend is across the country, and she has already given up on you. You have no money. So, tell me, what's your plan?" he pushes me against the wall this time with his body.

That familiar terror builds just before he used to hit me. This is it.

"Nowhere. I just want to go for a walk to clear my head," I state, but he can see right through me.

A sharp pain in the back of my head appears as I realize he's gripping my hair, and then he yanks it back against the wall. I raise my hands to my head to protect myself, but he continues to hold me against the wall with his body and slams the back of my head against it three more times. My vision blurs a little, but I refuse to lose consciousness.

My fight instinct has kicked in as I knee him in the balls. He lets go of me to grab himself and falls to his knees on the floor. It's my chance.

"You bitch!" he yells and grabs my leg as I try to run away.

I fall forward and twist my wrist on the impact. It hurts, but I can't think about it right now. I kick at his hand, and he lets go when I hit him. He's still in pain from my knee to his balls, so he's not able to get up quickly as I run out of the room. On my way to the door, I yank my phone off the charger, grab my purse from the wall, and pick up my shoes as I run out the front door. I don't look back or stop until I'm far enough away from the apartment and at a gas station with people around.

I run inside and find the bathroom quickly, locking the door. I look at myself in the mirror and I'm a mess. My hair is everywhere, so I pat it down and wipe away the tears in my eyes. There's nothing I can do about the puffiness, but I can at least try to make myself look a little presentable. I have no idea what I'm going to do when I leave this bathroom, but right now I know I can't go back there. I finally slip on my shoes and I pull out my phone, dialing Sierra's number.

My phone vibrates in my pocket, bringing me back to reality. It shows Bash is calling, but I hit ignore. I'm not going to fall into another toxic relationship. I can't. I'll be clear with Bash that we're over soon, but I can't talk to him right now. I lay on my bed and close my eyes, wishing my life wasn't the mess I've let it become.

CHAPTER TWENTY-ONE

BASH

It's been almost two weeks since Amelia walked out of my apartment. I've been texting and calling her every single day, but she never responds or answers. When she didn't show up for work the following Monday, I assumed she just needed time. Then Sierra made me aware she found a teaching job and quit. I'm crawling out of my skin, thinking about it. I can't stand the lack of communication in a relationship. It creates fucking problems that don't need to be there, like this one.

I understand she's upset, and she has every right to be, but if she'd talk to me, she'd understand it's not what she thinks. I wanted to explain it to Sierra so she could talk to her, but I'm not about to put her in the middle of this. I even came to terms that we may not work out, and I need to let her go, but I refuse to do that until she knows the truth. I can't have her thinking that I cheated on her. Not because it'll make me look bad, but so she knows it's not her. She's amazing. I honestly doubt I can do better than her.

I don't understand these feelings. Maybe they're just so intense because I haven't felt this way about anyone in a very long time, if ever at all. I don't want to lose her. I want to continue getting to know her and seeing where our relationship could go. If only I could get her to talk to me and give me a chance.

"You going to hide up here forever?" Jake stands at the bedroom door, asking.

Whenever we're in this house, and I'm in my old bedroom, it feels like I'm back in high school all over again. I have mixed feelings being here. Back in high school, I couldn't wait to get out of this house and go to college. As much as my father and I didn't get along, I had it good. Back then, I hated my life. I hated my dad. I'm still not exactly fond of my old man, but I understand him better.

"Is that an option?" I ask, only half joking.

Jake shrugs and sits at the end of the bed. "It always feels weird, doesn't it? Being back home. Not much has changed here, including our rooms."

I pick up a picture frame of the five of us from the last summer we had with Everly before everything went to shit. I look it over and admire how young and carefree we all were. We all had our shit going on, but on this day, it was like magic. We went ziplining to get Everly's mind off what was happening with her ex. It worked for the most part. Ziplining seems to make you forget your problems. Maybe I should go again.

Those smiling faces looking back at me taunt me. Look how good you all had it back then. Jake still smiles today, but it's fake, not like this picture. I see right through him, even though I don't point it out like I should. Even James is smiling in this picture. That's been a rarity to see in the past six years. With Everly back though, I can see it coming back too. I haven't seen Everly much, but I know she hasn't smiled that way in a while. Ben has become a lot more serious too, like his brother. Then there's me. Geez, when was the last time I looked that happy? When I'm with Amelia, that's when.

"Yeah, I kind of miss it," I say, placing the photo back down on the desk.

"Me too..." Jake says, looking at the ceiling, lost in thought.

Sitting next to him, I ask, "What's going on with you, man?"

"What do you mean?" he asks with that fake ass smile.

I point to his face. "That, right there. I can see through that fake smile."

He shakes his head. "Honestly? I don't know. I mean, it's all still the same, right? Dad's always on my case, and I'm never good enough. For him or a girl."

Damn my heart nearly breaks for him. I'm feeling like shit about the breakup with Amelia, but Jake has been hurting for a while. I blame my old man for this. Jake's right, he made us feel like we were never good enough, and apparently Jake believes that.

"You know that's not true, right? You're awesome Jake. Look at everything you do for the company, and I don't know how I'd do life without you. You'll find the right girl," I respond, trying not to get too emotionally deep into it right now.

Jake laughs and pats me on the shoulder. "Yeah, you're right. You couldn't live without me. With that, I'm going to tell you it's time you suck it up and go get your girl. Have fun tonight, but I'm sick of seeing you mope around. Go fix it."

I shake my head. "She refuses to talk to me."

"Then wait outside her work. Don't give her a choice anymore," he states.

"I don't want to push her…"

Jake interrupts. "She needs it. Bash, I haven't seen you so happy since you met her. Just like I can see James and Everly are meant for each other, I can see you and Amelia are. Don't let some stupid miscommunication ruin something great."

He's right. It is a stupid miscommunication and what we had was great. I'm not ready to let her go without a fight. Tomorrow, I'm going to wait for her outside the school she works at. Today, I'm going to enjoy time with my friends at my parents' Halloween party.

Jake and I part ways when I head downstairs. He said he needed to put on his makeup, which I'll be curious to see. James decided that everyone would dress as characters from *Once Upon A Time*. It was Everly's favorite tv show back in high school and she used to force us to watch it. I want to say I hated it, but I didn't. It was entertaining, at least.

So, I'm dressed up as Prince Charming. Dark red velvet cape, brown pants, vest, tall black boots, and all. I don't mind dressing up, but I wish Amelia was here. She would've been dressing up as Snow White, since those two are paired together in the show.

Jake is Rumpelstiltskin, so when I saw him in similar tight brown pants and leather boots like me, I thought it was a little underdone being it's Jake. Typically, he goes all out. I'm interested to see what he does with the makeup.

I find Ben and James already at the party in the corner of the room. They usually come early and offer their help to my parents. My parents always say no, go enjoy the party, but they ask every time.

I walk up and pat them both on the shoulder, looking them over. Ben is dressed as Robin Hood, and he dyed his hair. He looks more like James with his hair like that. His outfit is somewhat similar to mine, but his cape is dark green, and he has on a leather outfit with dark brown boots. It suits him. James is Hook, which means Everly must be Emma Swan. She's not here yet, though. She's going to die when she sees James in those tight black leather pants, vest, and long black leather coat. I'm thankful my pants aren't as tight as his.

We catch up for a bit until Jake joins us.

"You forgot something," Jake states, handing me a giant heavy ass sword.

"What the hell am I going to do with this?" I ask, lifting the thing up, trying to figure out how I'm going to carry it around.

"You hold it?" he asks, looking at me like I'm an idiot.

I shake my head, not complaining because it does complete the outfit. I look him over. He has on a long-sleeved silky shirt with a brown vest over it, along with even tighter brown leather pants and knee-high black boots. He overdid it on the makeup, because he looks just like Rumpelstiltskin in the show with the odd skin color, wrinkles, and all. He's holding a blade that looks just as real as the one he gave me. At least his is smaller.

James excuses himself to take a phone call while the rest of us continue to catch up like we didn't just see each other a few weeks ago. Ben grabs us some beers just before Everly joins our group.

"You guys look amazing!" Everly says loudly over the scary music playing.

"You're a perfect Emma Swan, Everly," Ben says, gesturing toward her outfit.

She makes a great Emma Swan, but her costume is modest. She's wearing dark blue skinny jeans with brown knee-high boots, similar to the rest of us. She has a red leather jacket over a gray tank top shirt. The blonde, wavy wig makes it all come together to look like her in the show.

Everly returns the compliment, "You all are perfect too, like wow. You guys went all out."

After she studies our costumes, she turns toward me to say, "So, where's Amelia? Is she dressed as Snow White?"

My smile instantly drops at the mention of Amelia. I didn't tell everyone that she wouldn't be here today. The only one who knew was Jake.

"She couldn't make it tonight," I reply.

Jake interrupts, "What he means to say is that he screwed up and they are in a fight."

Thanks Jake. I know what he's doing though, trying to give me more of a push to go fix things with Amelia. Standing here talking with Everly makes me feel a little guilty. I don't like that Amelia thinks I'm cheating on her with Everly. What if she somehow was here tonight and saw me with her?

Everly's friends, Ashley and Paige, come up to the group, distracting us. Ashley stands between Everly and Ben. I know Ashley used to have a crush on Ben, but I'm not sure if she still does. I watch them for a few moments to see her flirting with him. Okay, clearly, she does, and Ben is completely unaware.

I watch Jake check out Paige and whisper something to Everly. Whatever he says makes her smack his arm and say sternly, "She's always been hot, but no, Jake."

He puts up his hands in front of him and says, "I'm not going there."

Everly and I both shake our heads. Jake will probably flirt with Paige most of the night, but that seems to be all he does lately. I know I'm not with him all the time, but I haven't seen him go home with a girl in… well, it's been a long time.

Something catches Everly's attention, and she's not looking away. I don't need to look to know that James has come back into the room. The way Everly is staring at him makes me think they need some alone time immediately.

James wraps his arm around her waist and pulls her in for a kiss, which seems like it'll never end. Jake averts his eyes after a moment, and I can't help but feel a little angry with James for shoving this in his face. I get they are still having problems with each other and James wants to make it known Everly is his, but I'm protective of my brother.

After their little reunion, Ben drags them back into the group conversation as we all reminisce about the past. The fun college night we all shared gets brought up and I laugh.

I look at Everly and ask, "Do you still have a scar from when you caught me on fire?"

"Oh my gosh, yes! Look!" Everly lifts her shirt, showing us the scar, but James shoves it back down quickly.

He whispers something in her ear and they're not being discreet about wanting each other right here. Jake is looking annoyed, so I continue our conversation to distract everyone. I lift my sleeve to show my scar as well.

"You know, I'm pretty sure Everly just shouldn't be near fire," Ben says while pushing a candle that sits on a table next to us further away from her.

"What? I'm not dangerous when it comes to fire, it's fine," Everly says, feigning to be hurt.

Ben continues the conversation by describing how she burned his bangs off back in high school with a propane heater. She argues that those are just two instances, but then Jake brings up one that no one has heard before. Apparently, in her college days, when Jake was down there one summer, the power went out and she set a curtain on fire with candles. Needless to say, that one curtain ended up also catching Jake's pants on fire, another curtain on fire, and Everly's security guard, Declan's shirt on fire. Yeah, she shouldn't be around fire. I can't help myself as I laugh, hard.

Paige and Ashley come back after the story was told, making way for Everly and James to sneak off. Ashley is back to flirting with Ben, and Jake walks off to get another drink. I follow him and figure I'll use the rest of the night to drown my sorrows and prepare for confronting Amelia tomorrow.

Chapter Twenty-Two

AMELIA

It's the last day of my first week, and I'm just as exhausted as I was after the first week of working with Sierra. I've been trying to finish up the lessons that the prior teacher ended on, while figuring out what she has already taught.

The scheduling is also different from my old school. We have block schedules here, so I only have three classes to teach in a day. I have two classes with sophomores and one class with gifted juniors. I like the longer classes honestly because I get to spend more time getting to know the students and teaching the lessons versus rushing through it all and hoping they don't forget it by the next class. I'm not one to assign homework, unless it's a paper that they just didn't feel like working on in class. That's on them to use their class time wisely.

Anyway, I can tell my class with the juniors is going to be easy. They all seem to want to learn and put in the effort. The sophomores, on the other hand, are lazy and just want to have fun. I suppose I was like that at that age, so I get it. It's just annoying from this side.

I pack up my laptop and place it in my backpack, ready to go home and get some rest. I want nothing more than to sit on my couch like a bum and read a good book.

A quick knock sounds on the open door to my classroom. I look over to see Lawrance, another English teacher, leaning against the wall with his messenger bag over his shoulder. I smile at him and say, "Hey."

He smiles back. "Hey. Just checking in to see how your first week went."

I shake my head and give a defeated laugh. "It was rough, but good. They all seem like good kids. I just can't wait to teach my own lessons."

He pushes off the wall and replies, "Yeah, I came in when a teacher quit too. It's hard trying to figure out what they've already done and what they were planning to do next."

"Yes! You get it," I say, walking past him out the door and he follows.

"You have plans this weekend?" he asks.

"Plans with my book tonight and lesson plans all weekend. What about you?" I ask back.

"Just grading some papers and relaxing. Do you want to go out to dinner tonight and talk about your week? Or maybe coffee one morning this weekend?" he asks, looking unsure of himself.

Is he asking me out on a date or just being friendly? Lawrence has been great at helping me out this week, as he's right across the hall. It's easy to just pop my head in to ask him something. He also hasn't batted an eye at all with my clumsiness and craziness that comes my way.

I look him over, and he's cute with light brown, messy hair and brown glasses. He has to be in his late twenties, but I don't think he's older than that. Regardless, I'm not looking to date right now, especially someone I work with. Been there, done that.

Rather than just saying I want to stay in this weekend, I decide to be open and communicate with him like an adult. I tend to struggle with that, so I'm going to start here.

"Are you asking me on a date or just as coworkers?" I ask.

He looks a little flustered and replies, "On a date, but if you're not into that, then I'd love to just as coworkers."

I give him an I'm sorry smile before saying, "I'm not really looking to date right now. I just got out of a relationship and haven't processed it yet. I'd love to go maybe sometime next week as friends? I need to relax this weekend and continue getting settled into my apartment."

"Sure, that sounds good. Let me know if you need anything," he says before leaving my side to unlock his car.

Mine's parked a few cars down, so we say our goodbyes there, and I head to my car. Yes, my car. Despite many protests, Sierra bought me a car. I fought her on it, but she refused to listen, saying that I needed it to stay safe. That carrying around my backpack with my laptop in it would put a target on my back to get mugged. Since I couldn't promise her that's not true, I gave in. So here I am, with a new car from my best friend who has given me more than I deserve in my lifetime.

I freeze when I spot a familiar SUV parked beside my car. I shake my head and laugh at myself. Of course that's not Bash silly. There are probably thousands of this same car in this city.

I unlock my door when I see Bash round the front of the SUV, stalking toward me. My pulse picks up and my heart does some stupid dance in my chest that I don't even know what it's for. Nervousness? Sadness? Excitement? All of the above?

"Hey." He places his hand on my open door, not giving me an opportunity to get in and close it.

"Hey," I state.

"Amelia... can we please talk?" he pleads.

I inwardly groan. I don't want to talk to him. I don't want his excuses or to relive the hurt that I felt the day I found those messages. I just want to put the past behind us and pretend we never happened.

He steps closer and I inhale his scent, sandalwood. I close my eyes for a moment, breathing it in, feeling relaxed. God, I miss him. I do want to talk this through and work it out, but he lied and cheated on me. I'm not going to be with someone like that. I can't be with someone like that again.

I take a step back. "Bash... it's best if we don't."

He takes another step forward, placing his hand on my shoulder while my back is against the car. Flashbacks of the last time I saw my ex fly through my head, making me panic. I know Bash wouldn't hurt me, or I think he wouldn't, but my body doesn't know that. Maybe I don't either.

"Amelia…" he starts.

I interrupt him. "Bash, please just go. Please."

"No, I'm not leaving until we talk this through. I've given you two weeks," he states sternly, dropping his hand down my arm and gripping my wrist. The same wrist that still hurts from the day I left my ex.

My throat closes up, and I feel the tears form in my eyes. My mind is racing in fifty directions. I don't know what to do. I can't think, I can't focus. Placing my hand on his chest, I try to push him back, but I don't think I'm doing it hard enough. He doesn't even budge.

I didn't notice anyone else was around, but Wells pulls Bash back, away from me. My breathing is hard and rapid. The distance doesn't do much to fix that.

Wells' voice is calm. "Why don't you head to the car, and Amelia will call you when she's ready."

"Wha…" Bash begins, but Wells interrupts.

Wells' eyes narrow and his voice is firm when he says, "Go sit in the car."

Bash takes a quick glance at me before doing what Wells says, getting back into the SUV without any questions.

Wells voice becomes soft as he looks down at me and holds my car door wide open. "Bash is a good guy, Miss Hart. He would never hurt you. Take some deep breaths before driving home."

I'm still not sure exactly what's going on, but I feel a little calmer now. I nod toward Wells and sit in my car, taking a deep breath like he instructed.

"May I give you some advice?" he asks.

I have a feeling he'll give it to me regardless, so I just nod.

"You should go home and really think about what you want with Bash. I think for both of your sakes that you should at least talk to him and hear him out. Then you can decide from there. If you decide that you don't want to, then text him, making it clear you have no interest in talking to or seeing him again."

He continues to hold the door open, waiting for my response. Once again, I just nod.

He nods back. "Goodbye, Miss Hart."

"Goodbye Wells," I say as he closes the door.

He rounds my car and gets into the driver's seat of the SUV. I take a few deep breaths and calm down before I put the car in drive. They are still sitting there when I leave, but once I'm about to turn right out of the parking lot, I watch them drive off as well in the opposite direction.

Did they wait for me to make sure that I was okay? How did Bash find me? Did Sierra tell him where I worked? I get angry again but shake the thoughts out of my head. Sierra wouldn't have betrayed me like that, and she would've warned me Bash was coming.

By the time I get home, I've come to my decision. Wells is right. I need to talk to Bash. I was just thinking earlier about how

I need to be better at communicating. If I did it with Lawrence, I can do it with Bash. I have to do it.

After we talk it through, I'll be clear with him. I can't be with someone who talks to another girl like that, even if he wants to sit here and deny that he was cheating with her. I also just can't be in a relationship right now. I plan to search for a therapist this weekend that I can talk to. After that interaction with Bash, I know I need one.

I know he wouldn't have hurt me, but my body had a mind of its own. I felt like I was suffocating, and I didn't know what to do. I felt like I was back in that apartment with Jayden and trapped. Sometimes I wonder what would have happened if I hadn't kneed him in the balls that day. Would I even be alive? Would he have killed me? What if I had gone back just like all the other times I did? I shake the thoughts out of my head. This is why I need a therapist and can't be in a relationship right now.

Making it back to my apartment, I plop myself on the couch with my arm laying over my eyes. I sigh and look at my phone. I'll call him later, but first, I need a quick nap.

CHAPTER TWENTY-THREE

BASH

Sitting in the passenger seat as Wells drives, I'm trying hard to control my temper right now. Wells never interrupts me, so when he did, I knew he had a good reason. I listened to him and got in the car without a word. Damn, I wanted to fight him on it though. I've been waiting two weeks to talk to Amelia, and that was my chance. He just cost me my chance, and I don't know why.

Fuck it. I'm done holding my tongue. "Why?"

He glances at me and then back at the road. He knows what I'm asking.

Sighing, he replies, "She was scared, Bash. She needed space."

My damn heart stops as I think about what he just said. I noticed her tense up and breath quicken, but I didn't think she was actually scared.

"Scared of me?" I ask calmly.

He shrugs his shoulders. "I don't know. You told me her ex was abusive. She looked like she was about to have a panic attack.

I didn't want you to push her. When people feel trapped, they do things they don't mean to."

He's right, I would've pushed her. I was pushing her to talk to me, but damn it. I didn't mean to scare her. I shouldn't have done that, but I don't know what else to do. We need to talk about this. I can't move on until we talk.

"What do I do now?" I ask, defeated.

"Wait," he states, like it's that simple.

"For what? The rest of my life? She's never going to come to me on her own," I say, looking out the window, frustrated.

"She will."

"Why do you think that?" I ask with a little hope in my voice.

"Because she still cares about you. She's just been hurt by her ex and now she feels hurt by you. She'll want to eventually talk about it. Just give her a little more time," he states again, like it's that easy.

I shake my head and stare out the window the rest of the drive home, wishing I would've done something, anything, differently. At this point, I just want her to talk to me. I just want to tell her my side, and she can break up with me if she wants to. It'll suck, but I can handle that. What I can't handle is thinking about her day and night, sucking at my job. It's torture. I've had to avoid Sierra at work too, which is hard when you work so closely with someone. It's not her fault. She's been really good at pretending she doesn't hate me for hurting Amelia.

The moment I walk through the front door, my phone rings. It's Amelia.

I answer it as quickly as possible. "Hello?"

"Hey," she says, her voice quiet.

"Hey," I reply nervously.

The silence is deafening. I want to say something, but I don't want to ruin this. She called me. I need to be patient, just like Wells said.

She finally breaks the silence. "I... I'm sorry about earlier. I wasn't expecting you to show up at my work and..."

She pauses, so I jump in. "No, I'm sorry. I shouldn't have just shown up like that."

I hear her sigh. "You're right. We need to talk."

"When?" I ask, hoping she means soon.

"Are you free tonight?"

"I am. Tell me where and I'll be there," I state, trying not to sound too eager, but I know I fail.

"There's a restaurant down the street from the school that I've been wanting to try," she says.

"Send me the address and I'll be there."

I don't care that we literally just got back from driving there. I'll drive twenty hours if it means I get to see and talk to her.

"Can I ask for one thing?" she asks, sounding uncertain.

"Anything."

"Could you... could you bring Wells? He doesn't have to sit with us, but just close by?" She acts like she's asking for a million dollars.

I keep my voice even. "Wells will be there."

"Okay, thank you. I'll see you in a bit." She hangs up the phone.

Not even a minute later, my phone dings with a text from her with an address attached. It's an Italian restaurant that I've never heard of before. Even if she didn't ask for Wells to come, I would've brought him anyway. My heart sinks a little, thinking about how she doesn't want to be alone with me. That she trusts Wells more than me.

Amelia's sitting across the table from me at the empty Italian restaurant. For being so late on a Friday night, it's weird it's so slow. We did a little research before getting here and it has good enough reviews, so I'm not sure why. I shake my head. What does it matter? Amelia's here, and she's finally willing to talk.

Wells came in with me and said a quick hello to Amelia before taking a seat at the bar where he can see us, and she can see him. She looked relieved when she saw him. It hurts a little to know she really doesn't trust me.

We still haven't said a word to each other when the waiter arrives to get our drink order. She gets water with lemon, and I ask for the same. When the waiter leaves, she's staring at the menu like she's really concentrating on figuring out what she's going to get.

"Anything look good?" I ask her, breaking the silence between us.

She places the menu down on the table. "Honestly? It all does, but I'm not that hungry right now. I don't know why I picked this place."

"You said you've been wanting to try it," I repeat her words back to her.

"Yeah, I did... I'm too nervous to eat," she whispers.

I instinctively reach for her hand on the table to comfort her, but she pulls it away. I place my hand back on my lap. That was a stupid move.

"How about you just get whatever looks good, and you can take it home for later?" I ask instead of saying it because I don't want it to sound like a demand.

"Yeah, sure," she says as she studies the menu again.

We're silent once more until the waiter takes our orders and removes the menus. She doesn't have anything to hide behind now.

"Do you want me to start, or you?" I ask her.

I've been trying to let her lead this conversation, but I have a feeling she's not going to actually start it. There's no point being here if we're not going to talk about it, even if I love being in her company.

She sighs. "You said you wanted to explain the texts, that it wasn't what it looked like. So go ahead and explain."

She already has in her head that I cheated on her. I'm going to tell her the truth, but I'm worried she's not going to believe me.

"I've known Everly since we were kids. She'd stay every summer at the Crawford's house after her mother died. That's my best friend James' house. Everly had a tough go at it, especially since her senior year of high school. She dated my brother, Jake, for a few days and then they broke up. Honestly, I still don't think he's fully over her. They had a thing for a bit in college, too. Anyway, her and James were together too, and they broke up when she went to college, but they're back together now..." I say all this and pause to look at her reaction.

She looks at me with furrowed brows, like she's confused. I know I'm not good at telling stories, but I just want to make it clear that I have no feelings for her, and she's taken.

I continue. "Sorry, I know I can be long winded explaining things. Anyway, she's James' girlfriend. During her senior year, she went through a lot of bad shit that no one should ever have to go through. I don't like sharing this about her, but I feel you need to know to understand... She tried to kill herself, but thankfully, she survived."

I pause again to see her face has turned from confusion to sadness.

She doesn't say anything, so I continue. "She was in a really bad place and after that, the four of us, James, Ben, Jake, and I, took on different roles. My role was to boost her confidence and self-esteem. I started texting her every single day, just reminding her how amazing she was and how much she was needed and wanted here. This continues more than six years later, but the frequency has died down to about once a week. The messages you saw that night were about how we all met up with her for the first time since she left. I know it didn't look like it, but she's like my little sister. James knows about the messages, too. It's not something I meant to hide from anyone, especially you."

She takes a sip of her water and still doesn't say anything. She looks like she's thinking over what I said. I can't tell if she believes me or not. The fact this is the honest truth kills me that she might not believe me.

"So, the two of you have never been anything more than friends?" she asks skeptically.

"She's my sister. I will always consider her my little sister," I state.

"You've never kissed her or anything?" she asks to clarify.

"Never."

She nods. "I believe you."

I didn't know how much I needed to hear those three words until she said them, and a giant weight lifts off my chest. It killed me knowing she thought I was cheating on her.

"Amelia, I'm sorry I wasn't upfront with you before about Everly," I state sincerely.

"I know," she whispers.

"What does this mean for us?" I ask, not wanting to push her, but not wanting to be in limbo anymore.

She gives me a sad smile. "I appreciate your honesty, Bash, and I'm not upset with you anymore. I think what you do for her and have done for her is a really great thing. You are so kind and an amazing person, but all of this showed me that I'm just not ready for a relationship right now."

The hope that I had moments ago deflated with those words. She doesn't want to be with me.

"Okay," I state, not knowing what else to say.

She looks at me with pity. "Bash, it's not that I don't want to be with you, but I just can't. I... I'm going to be completely honest. My ex really messed with me, and it wasn't even that long ago. I got really upset when I thought you were cheating on me, just like he did. I also don't like how I fear you. Knowing you would never hurt me doesn't change how my body reacts in certain situations. I need to figure that out. I need to fix myself before I can be with someone."

While what she says makes sense, it still feels like she's turning me down. It fucking hurts. I want to be there for her when she's upset. I want to be there for her while she figures things out, but I understand where she's coming from.

"Are you sure you can't do all that with me in the picture? I promise I won't push you. I'll just be there for you when you need me, and I'll be patient," I plead with her.

"Bash..." she states with tears forming in her eyes.

"Amelia... I really care about you. I just want to be there for you. Everything is so much better when you're around," I state.

A tear slips down her cheek as the food arrives. She gives a smile when the waiter places her lasagna down in front of her, but she doesn't lift her head to make eye contact with him.

Once he walks away, she says, "I don't think so Bash. I really need to concentrate on myself. My ex hurt me, and I never took the time to fix myself. I've been pretending what happened with him never happened. I mean, he still has all my stuff. I left San Diego with the clothes on my back, phone, and purse..."

I interrupt her. "What do you mean he still has your stuff?"

She looks away and back again, embarrassed. "He threatened if I left him that he'd take all of it. He was on the lease and would claim it was all his. My books, clothes, everything..."

I'm so angry right now, but I try to push it down for her sake. Not only am I angry at her ex for keeping her things, but I'm angry that I never knew this until now. I take a deep breath and let it out.

"You'll get your things back," I state, not explaining that I'll be the reason she gets them back. I have a feeling she would argue that point.

She nods. "I will, but that's just one thing I need to figure out. I have to take some time and do this myself. I'm sorry, Bash."

I nod, even though I want to fight this. I want to argue with her. It'll be better if we do this together, but I can't. I don't know what she's gone through with her ex, but I need to trust that she knows what's best for herself.

"Okay. I understand, but Amelia..." I say while trying one more time to put my hand on hers. This time, she doesn't pull away. "I'm here, okay? I'm going to wait for you. When you're ready to try this again, text me. If you need something, anything, just text me. Okay?"

She nods as more tears slip down her face. I don't push her to say anything, and I just let her go. She heads to the restroom to clean herself up while I get her a to go box and pay for the meal. I walk her out to her car and hug her before we part ways.

I'm not happy with the outcome of this conversation, but I'm not going to give up on her. She's different from any girl I've ever been with. I know we weren't together long, but that's all I needed to know that my life without her in it sucks. I'm going to keep trying to be there for her, and I'm going to wait until she's ready. I'm not giving up until she tells me flat out that she doesn't ever want to see me again.

CHAPTER TWENTY-FOUR

AMELIA

It's been two weeks since Bash and I talked. I miss him. He sends me sweet texts every couple of days. I imagine they are similar to the ones he sends Everly, and I can see why he does it. They are a kind pick me up and even though sometimes I don't believe what he says, it's nice to hear it. It's nice that someone thinks I'm beautiful and worth it.

After his first text, he made it clear he would stop if I told him to. I didn't tell him to. I haven't responded to any of his messages, but I don't know if I want him to stop. I really like him, and we had fun together.

Sierra also brought me a surprise the other day. It was a package for me, from Bash. Apparently, it arrived at her place the day after I left Bash's apartment upset about the texts, but she didn't want to give it to me at that time. I'm thankful because I probably would have thrown it away.

I opened it to find a bracelet sitting inside and not just any bracelet, but my bracelet. The one I lost on the beach, that I hadn't gotten around to telling Sierra I lost. There was a note inside explaining that he had a team searching for it, and it finally turned up. I can't believe he remembered it, and he put so much effort into finding it. I'll have to thank him the next time I see him. I'm not ready to text him yet.

I found a therapist named Liberty, and I've seen her four times already. Thankfully, I only pay a small copay for each session. She's really great, and I feel like she's helped me a lot already. I'll only be going to weekly sessions soon, but she thought I would benefit right now from going twice a week. I've been completely honest with her about everything in my life. There's a lot to work through, but I think we'll get there.

Liberty convinced me to join my coworkers for a fun night out. She thinks it's great that I have Sierra, but said I need to make connections to the ones I'll be working closely with if I intend to stick around. We haven't talked too much about Bash yet, but she agreed it's good to concentrate on myself right now. Though she thinks that if I want to talk to Bash, I should. That I shouldn't overthink it like I do with everything in my life.

So, Liberty is the reason that I'm standing here with a sharp object in my hand. That sharp object so happens to be an axe. An axe that I'm supposed to be throwing at a target on the wall. I don't know whose idea it was to meet up at an axe throwing place, but here we are.

I've watched each of my coworkers take turns and throw this deadly object at the wall. Now it's my turn. My heart races as I step forward and try not to fall on my face. I don't want to embarrass myself in front of them on our first night out. I lift the axe with both hands over my head, and it's much heavier than I thought it'd be. I step forward and throw it as hard as I can toward the target.

At least, I thought I threw it at the target. I did not. In fact, I threw it at the floor, which has a rubber mat. It bounces off said rubber mat, and I'm certain at this moment I'm going to die. My brain plays the scene in slow motion as the axe bounces off the floor, hits the wall, and bounces back toward me.

I stop breathing and dodge to the left as it flies past my face, missing me by a centimeter. I'm literally shaking and laughing as everyone else stares at me with stunned looks on their faces. It's fine. I'm fine. I'm alive.

"Holy shit Amelia," Rachel says as she pulls me to the side, looking me over.

"I've never seen that happen before," Lawrence says quietly.

"That was amazing!" Dan exclaims.

All I can do is continue to laugh as the near-death experience replays in my head. Dan slides up beside me, holding out his phone. He caught the whole thing on video. Before we can watch the replay, one of the workers comes up to us and spends the next minute scolding me for the way I threw the axe.

I don't feel like I did anything wrong, and my coworkers back me up. The instructor that was teaching us how to throw only spent two minutes with us and acted like he needed to go get his next fix of whatever he was high on. Needless to say, we leave the venue and decide to head to a bar instead.

By the time we get a table at the nearest bar, the adrenaline from the incident wears off. I'm now feeling embarrassed, especially since Dan keeps replaying the video for everyone to see. After the second time, I stopped watching. Okay, so the axe was a lot further away from me than I thought it was, but it still could've killed me!

"Can we forget this ever happened?" I groan.

All three stare at me before Rachel answers, "Um, no. That was amazing."

I place my face in my hands and shake my head. I can't believe this happened. They know I'm clumsy and weird stuff happens to me because they've experienced it firsthand at work, but to see it happen when we are hanging out... I feel like I'm never going to make actual friends.

"Seriously, that was pretty cool. We like hanging out with you, Amelia," Lawrence reassures.

"Thanks guys. I'm glad you got a good laugh out of it, at least."

As we get our second round of drinks, I want nothing more than to tell Bash about tonight. He would also get a kick out of it. After the third round, I decide to go for it. My therapist said if I want to talk to him, I should.

"Can you send me that video?" I ask Dan.

He grins. "Of course."

My phone dings with his message, and I save it to my phone. I type out a text to Bash with the video.

Bash doesn't respond again, so I place the phone down on the table.

"Who did you send it to?" Rachel asks.

"My old boss." I shrug and finish my third drink.

"Your old boss?" Lawrence looks at me questionably.

"Yeah, I thought he'd get a kick out of it. I'm pretty clumsy, as you all know, so he experienced a lot of my crazy."

"Does this old boss happen to be more than just a boss?" Rachel asks, waggling her eyebrows.

I shake my head. "It's not like that."

That's not a lie. Currently, he is just my old boss. We're not dating or anything. We're friends… I think. Dang it, I really want to be friends with him. No, I want more. What am I doing?

Dan changes the topic, and I'm thankful. I'm pretty sure Rachel was about ten seconds away from getting the truth out of me, and that's not really something I want to talk about right now.

My phone dings again with another text from Bash.

My heart races and embarrassment creeps up again.

Bash's responses aren't immediate again, so I continue talking to my friends for a while. I'm feeling pretty tipsy, so I know I need to get an Uber back home. I drove here thinking that I'd only have one drink, not three. Rachel's brother is coming to pick her up, and he offered to drive us all home, but I don't want to be an inconvenience. I can afford an Uber.

As I pull up the app, I notice a text from Bash that I missed.

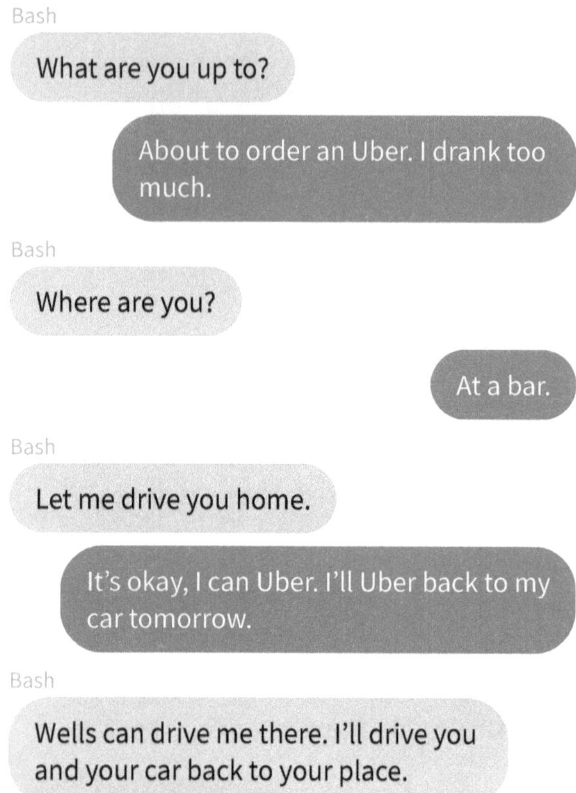

I stop and think about it for a minute. That makes a lot of sense and would save me two Uber trips, but that means I would have to see Bash. Do I want to see Bash? My rapid heart rate is an indication that I do. I miss him. A lot. Is it a good idea to see him tonight, though? Especially when I've had a few drinks?

I mean, I almost died tonight. How can it get any worse?

Okay.

Bash

I'll be there in five.

"My brother just pulled up. You sure you don't want a ride?" Rachel asks, pulling me out of my conversation with Bash.

"Yeah, I'm okay. I have someone coming to get me," I say, not wanting to give up who.

"Alright. I'll see you at work Monday," she says, giving me a hug, then turning to my two other coworkers. "You guys coming?"

"Should we stay to make sure she gets off okay?" Lawrence asks them, but is looking at me.

"Seriously, I'll be fine. He'll be here any minute."

"Oh, so it's a he?" Rachel beams.

Ugh, I screwed up. I don't respond to her.

"Oh, come on. It's the old boss, isn't it?"

I still don't answer.

"Alright, alright. We'll talk about this in private when the boys aren't around." She grins.

Lawrence looks at me like he's concerned and... disappointed? My heart sinks. I know he asked me out on a date, but I can't imagine that he actually likes me. At least, not enough to care if I have another guy picking me up.

"I had a really good time. See you guys Monday," I say.

I watch as they leave the bar. I hit the bathroom and then head outside to wait for Bash. It's been five minutes, so he should be here soon.

Wait... I didn't tell him where I was...

"Hey," Bash says from behind, startling me.

"Jesus!" I slap my hand over my heart.

"No, it's just me. You're not dead. The axe did miss your head," he says with a tentative smile.

I stare at him. Then I laugh, hard. So hard that I'm thankful I went to the bathroom before I came out here, otherwise I would've peed my pants.

He laughs too. "You really are drunk."

I shake my head. "Not drunk, just tipsy."

"Then I like tipsy Amelia."

I straighten up from my laughing fit and study him. He looks good. His hair is styled perfectly without a strand out of place. He's wearing a white long-sleeved button-down shirt with black dress pants and shoes. He looks so professional, even on a Friday night.

"Where were you tonight?" I ask.

"Down the street, having dinner with my brother."

"Dressed like that?" I ask.

He smirks. "It wasn't a cheap restaurant."

Oh. Of course. He's a billionaire, and obviously, so is his brother. They would eat out at fancy, super expensive restaurants. I bet he had on a full suit and his jacket is sitting in the car right now.

"What's wrong?" he asks.

Huh? I must be looking at him in a weird way, so I quickly ask, "How did you know where I was?"

His smile fades. "I may have looked at your location."

"I stopped sharing my location with you after... you know," I say.

We were sharing our location with each other just like I do with Sierra, but the moment I turned my phone back on after what happened, I stopped sharing it with him. It just felt like a good fuck you moment.

"I have other ways to track you," he states seriously.

A shiver runs down my spine. It's not necessarily a bad one. He cares enough to figure out other ways to keep track of me. I guess that's how he found where I worked. Normally, I would be really upset about this invasion of privacy. I'd be scared if it were anyone but him, especially my ex, but it's not. It's Bash.

I hand him my car keys. "Take me home big boy."

What the fuck did I just call him?

"Big boy?" he laughs.

I facepalm myself. Seriously, why do I say stupid shit?

"I'm drunk, let's go."

He laughs even harder. "You just said you weren't drunk, you're tipsy."

I wave him off. "Yeah, that. You taking me home or what?"

"Yeah, I'm taking you home." He places his hand on my lower back, leading me to my car and opening the door for me. This is going to be the longest fifteen-minute drive ever.

Chapter Twenty-Five

BASH

I can't sleep. After driving Amelia back to her apartment, Wells brought me home. I already knew where she lived, so she didn't have to tell me. I was surprised she didn't bring it up, but I already came clean about knowing her location. Maybe I have a problem. I check it almost every hour of the day, minus when I'm sleeping.

She let me walk her up to her door, and then she did something I never thought she would. She invited me in. Then I did something I never thought I would. I declined. This is why I'm not able to sleep. I keep going over it in my head, regretting saying no, but then coming to terms with it being the right thing to do.

She was drunk, regardless of how many times she denied it. I didn't want her to regret inviting me in, even though I never would have taken advantage of her in that state. I want her to invite me in when she's sober and there's nothing clouding her judgement. Regardless, tonight showed me something impor-tant. She still wants me.

My phone vibrates on my end table. I pick it up to see who's texting me this late at night.

I grin at my phone like an idiot. How can one simple text from a girl make me feel like this?

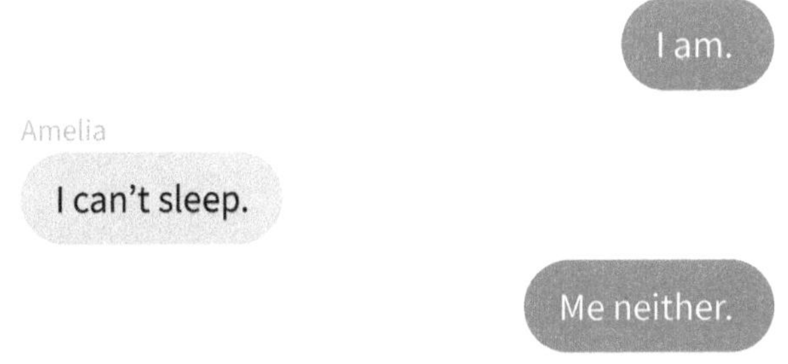

There's a pause in her response, but I keep staring at my phone, just waiting for those three little dots to pop up. They do.

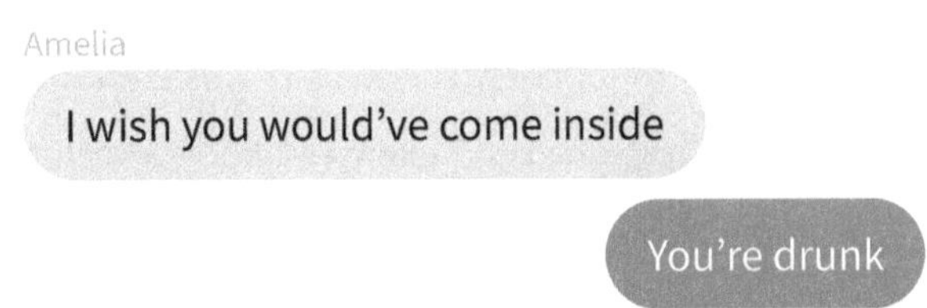

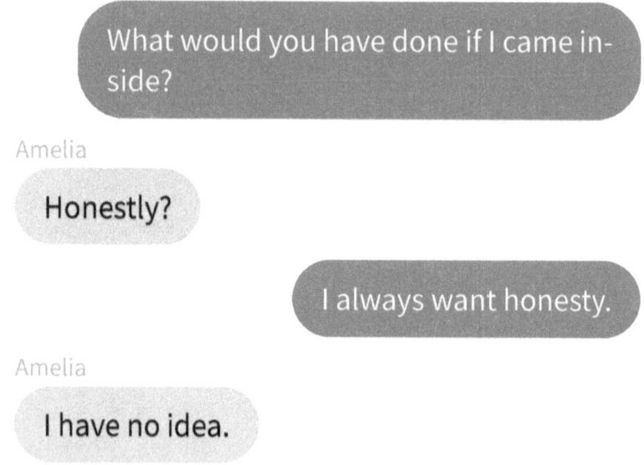

I can't help but laugh at her, insisting she wasn't drunk, but she's right. The alcohol is surely out of her system now.

I grin at my phone and then realize what it is that I'm feeling. I'm falling for this girl. I've had a lot of emotions when it comes to women, but never anything like this. Lust has been there, but it never lasted more than the few times I had sex with them. I never wanted to get to know any of them better. I had a long-term girlfriend once, and I thought that I loved her. I can now see that I loved the idea of her. Amelia... Amelia is different. I've barely known her, but I feel like we've known each other forever.

If anyone would've asked me a year ago if I believed in soul mates, I would've said no. If they asked me now... I'd have to say yes. I've felt this odd connection with her since the moment I laid eyes on her. It's like our souls were reaching for each other.

I shake my head to get those sappy thoughts out. I'm not a sappy person, but damn, do I miss Amelia.

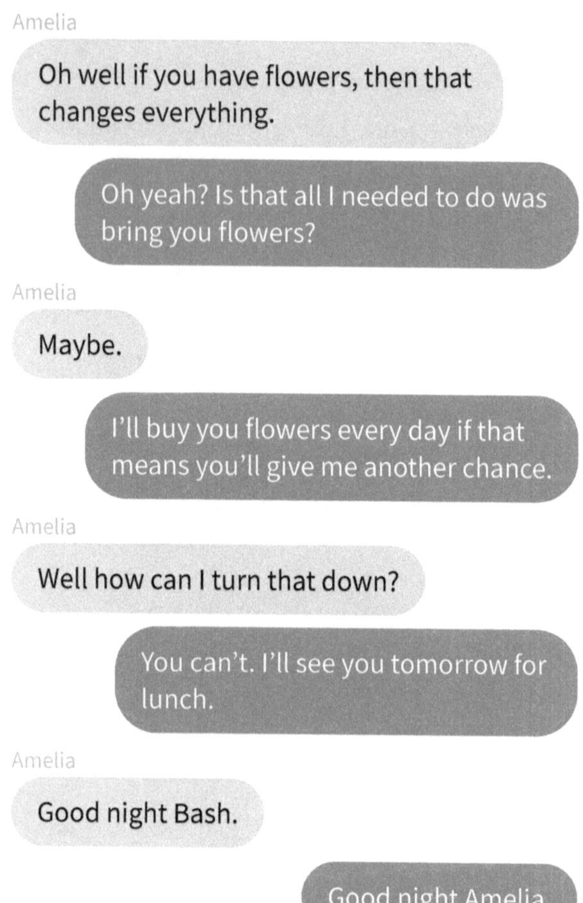

I turn the screen off on my phone, so I'm not tempted to continue texting her. She needs sleep, and so do I. I have to figure out how I'm going to win her back. She's giving me another chance, and I'm not going to fuck it up.

Well, I fucked it up. I'm an hour late, and I didn't have time to get her flowers. I probably should've stopped to get them for her, but I didn't want to be any later than I already was. Hank called Wells to let him know there was another breach in our system. It seems like it's the same guy, but he still can't pinpoint who it is. Hank is the best of the best, so it's concerning if he's not able to figure it out.

So that led to me going into an emergency meeting at the office to discuss the issue. My security team is trying to put even more security in place with the accounts, but there is only so much they can do.

As we pull up in front of her apartment, my phone rings with a call from Tim.

"Hello?" I answer.

Wells looks at me, and I give him a nod. I don't even need to speak for him to know that means go get Amelia. We're already so late. I don't want her waiting any longer than necessary.

"You have a minute?" he asks.

No, I really don't, but for him I always do.

"What's up?"

"We've had another security breach. Have you had any more issues?" he asks.

I groan. "Yeah, I've been dealing with that all day."

"Any leads?"

"Nope." I don't need to ask if he does, because he wouldn't have asked me first if he did.

"Me neither. Who is this person and why are they targeting us?"

"Not sure. It makes me wonder if it's someone we both know or if it's just a coincidence since we're connected with so many things," I ponder.

Wells opens the back door and Amelia slides in. She gives me a shy smile as she settles in the seat beside me. I nod toward her, apologizing with my eyes.

"If you find anything, let me know," Tim states.

"Same. We'll talk later," I state, hanging up the phone without a goodbye.

Amelia looks at me with concern. I was expecting her to be irritated that I was late and wasn't the one to come to her door to get her.

"Hey," I say cautiously.

Her eyebrows furrow. "Everything okay?"

I run my hand through my hair and sigh. "It's been a long day."

"We can postpone the date if you want," she whispers.

"No. I want to go out. I've missed you," I say sincerely.

She smiles. "Me too."

I hold her hand on her lap and am happy she doesn't pull away. We're quiet for most of the ride to the restaurant. I haven't apologized yet for being late, but I will.

When we arrive, she stays seated for me to open the door for her. I'm glad she remembers. Wells drives off as we enter the restaurant. I give the hostess my name and she brings us upstairs to a private room.

After we're seated, Amelia says, "When you said we're going for lunch, I thought that meant pizza or something."

I laugh. "Would you prefer that?"

She shakes her head. "No. I mean... Honestly, this," she waves her hand around the room, "makes me a little uncomfortable."

"I don't want you uncomfortable. We can go somewhere else," I state sincerely.

"No! Seriously, this is great. I'm just not used to it."

I nod. "I promise it's not as bad as it seems. I just really wanted a restaurant with a private room for us."

"It's nice. Beautiful here."

She stops talking and picks up her menu. The waitress comes by to take our drink orders and leaves us quickly. It feels like it's been forever and she's still looking at the menu, like she's memorizing it for an exam.

"See anything you like?" I ask, concerned she may not like anything on the menu.

When she puts down her menu, she blushes. "I mean... do you have any recommendations?"

"Nothing sounds good, huh?" I ask.

"It's not that... I mean... I don't know," she rambles.

I laugh. "Talk to me."

She clears her throat as she gets the courage to say what's on her mind. "I don't eat fancy foods and all this is fancy. There's a kid's section with chicken tenders and fries, which sounds amazing."

I place my hand on hers. "Get the chicken tenders."

Her voice becomes high pitched. "Bash! I can't get chicken tenders at a place like this! And look…" she points to the menu, "it's forty dollars for a kid's meal!"

I shake my head. "Amelia… stop looking at prices when you're around me. I know you're not used to it, but I want to spoil you. I have more money than I know what to do with and that's with giving a lot away. Let me spend it on you."

She doesn't respond, as she's processing what I just said. The waitress comes back, and I notice Amelia fumbling through the menu again like she's trying to quickly figure out anything but the tenders to order.

I go first. "You know, those chicken tenders sound great. Do you think I could get an adult version of the kid's meal?"

The waitress smiles at me. "Of course. What type of sauce would you like?"

I think for a moment. Amelia seemed to like honey mustard when we ordered them for room service. "Honey mustard."

"And for you?" the waitress asks, turning toward Amelia.

"I think I'll have the same as him," she states shyly.

"Of course. It'll be out in a few minutes. Let me know if you need anything else."

She walks away, and Amelia looks at me like she's mad, or pretending to be mad.

"What?" I ask innocently.

"Why would you get that?"

Shrugging my shoulders, I say, "Because they sounded good."

She shakes her head. "You could've gotten a big juicy steak or seafood, but you chose chicken tenders?"

"Like I said, they sounded good when you mentioned them."

Leaning back in her chair, she studies me and smiles. I don't know exactly what's going through her head, but I just want her happy. I could tell she wasn't going to be comfortable ordering chicken tenders, and I wanted her to get what she wanted. If I'm being honest, I don't typically eat foods like that. It won't hurt to every once in a while.

I move onto another topic. "I want to apologize for being late and not having time to bring you flowers. Some things came up at work, but that's no excuse."

"It's okay, it happens," she says sincerely.

"Thank you for being understanding," I say.

We spend the rest of the date talking about her new job and Sierra's new assistant. I can tell she misses working with her best friend, but she seems to love teaching. I want her to do what makes her happy and not have to worry about money. I think this date went well, and we're moving in the right direction to becoming a couple again.

I invited her to Thanksgiving with my family and friends, but she's going to San Diego to visit her parents. I hoped she'd offer for me to come with her, but she didn't. I would've hated missing out with my family, but I would've so I could spend it with her. I'm realizing I'd do a lot for this woman that I never thought I'd do before.

Chapter Twenty-Six

AMELIA

I honestly never wanted to set foot back in San Diego, but here I am. I flew in yesterday, and my flight back is tomorrow night. I don't want to spend longer than I need to here. I thought my parents would be out of state or even the country, but they aren't.

They don't have a ton of money, but they try to spend time together doing experiences they couldn't do when I was living at home. Again, I feel like I've never been anything but an inconvenience to them. I know they never wanted me, but I tried to be a good kid. Heck, I'm clearly still trying to get their approval because I caved and came to San Diego to spend time with them for Thanksgiving.

Thankfully, it's just the three of us. My parents have a lot of friends, but they don't have family around. I think that was difficult for them too. If they wanted to go out, they typically had to hire a babysitter or rely on a friend to watch me. They are proud people, so they rarely ask for help.

I had Sierra for a year in high school, but my parents were concerned when she went off to college. They didn't think a sophomore should be hanging around a college student so much. Sierra was a great friend and had a good head on her shoulders, but my parents have always been blinded by biases and what they think to be true.

"Are you done with the green bean casserole?" my mom asks, stepping beside me to look.

"Yeah, I just finished. What next?" I ask.

"Start the sweet potato casserole next. They can bake together," she says while fetching me the ingredients.

I've always wanted to help my mom cook for Thanksgiving, even if it's just the three of us. We usually cook and maybe talk about a few things, mostly about her. Rarely does she care much about my life. If she asks, it typically turns back to being about her.

As I'm smashing the canned yams, she asks, "So, how's it going in New York?"

I smile. "Good. I really like it there. I get to hang out with Sierra and my coworkers are really nice. I love my students and where I live. It was a good move."

She shakes her head. "I still don't see why you had to move across the country though."

Yep, there it is. I just told her I'm really happy, but she doesn't care.

Shrugging, I add, "I needed a change of scenery. There wasn't much left here for me when I left Jayden."

"Do you still talk to him?" she asks.

"No, and I don't intend to."

"Well I don't see why not. You two were together for so long. It's hard to believe you just threw all that away," she states, peeling a potato.

I force my anger to stay put and respond, "He's the one that threw it away, really. It doesn't matter, we're over, and I'm happy now."

She looks at me skeptically. "Did you find another boy?"

I want to laugh at her using the term boy. Bash is not a boy. Jayden would be considered a boy if you compared him to Bash.

"I've met someone, yeah," I say quietly.

"What's his name?"

"Bash," I state and don't elaborate.

"Bash what?"

"Hale. His real name is Sebastian Hale."

She drops the peeler and stares at me, clearing her throat. "This doesn't happen to be the same Sebastian Hale that is Sierra's boss, does it?"

I look at her, confused. "How do you know who Sierra's boss is?"

She waves her hand in the air like she's saying whatever. "Of course I looked into everything. Your father and I worry about you, so we wanted to know where you'd be working and who you were working for when you took the position with Sierra."

I barely told them anything about it. We rarely talk and the only thing I told her was the company name, Hale Financial

Solutions, and I'd be Sierra's assistant. She would have really had to do some research to find this out, and she remembered his name.

I shrug my shoulders. "Well, yeah, that's him."

"Oh, honey..." she says with a concerned voice.

"What?" I ask.

"He's a billionaire with a large company. I think you should let this one go and find a nice man like you," she states.

"What does that mean?" I ask, annoyed.

She shakes her head. "Like a teacher at your school."

She's missing my question. "Why couldn't I have Bash?"

Looking at me with pity, she says, "Because of what I just said. He could have anyone, and I'm sure he has a lot of women in his life. I don't want you to get hurt."

It's not often that I stand up to my mother or even show my annoyance, but it's hard to hold it in now. She's my mom. She shouldn't be sitting here telling me I'm not good enough for a man like Bash. I know she doesn't believe in me, but she could pretend.

I break. "So you're telling me I'm not good enough for him? Got it."

She gasps. "No, I didn't say that. I just... I know what those men with money are like, and you don't want that. Jayden was a hard-working man, and he took care of you. He loved you."

Are you kidding me right now? I know that I didn't tell them exactly what happened between Jayden and me, but that doesn't matter. She should be on my side, no matter what. She should be supporting me with what I want to do with my life and who I want to be with. All she has ever done my entire life is judge me and tell me I'm not good enough. I'm not good enough for them, for my profession, and apparently now for Bash. I can't do this anymore.

I throw the utensil on the counter and walk away.

"Where are you going?"

"For a walk," I state as I walk out of the kitchen, out the front door, slamming it.

I need to clear my head. I can't do this right now. Walking a few houses down, I stop suddenly with a sharp pain in my foot. Ow! Lifting my foot, I find a large piece of glass on the bottom. Apparently, I forgot to put my shoes on before leaving the house in my fit of rage, and now I'm regretting it because I just stepped on glass.

I look around to find a couple more pieces on the sidewalk. Sitting down where it's clear, I carefully remove the shard. I wince at the pain and at the blood gushing down my foot. Great. If I had my car here, I'd have a first aid kit in it, but I flew to San Diego.

I'm shrugging off my cardigan to use as a wrap when a familiar voice rings out on the sidewalk, giving me chills.

"Amelia?" Jayden asks, crouching down beside me.

No... No... This can't be happening right now. My mother thinks I'm not good enough for anything or anyone, blood is gushing from my foot, I'm in pain, and my ex is now beside me on the sidewalk. What the fuck did I do to deserve this sort of karma?

"I'm fine," I state before he can even ask.

"You're bleeding. Hang on," he says, jogging back toward his car, which is parked in my parents' driveway.

Are you serious? I just want to scream, but I don't want to make a scene in front of all the neighbors while they are just trying to enjoy their Thanksgivings in peace. I close my eyes and take a few deep breaths, like my therapist taught me to do.

Jayden comes running back with a first aid kit, sitting on the sidewalk with me. He takes out an alcohol pad and cleans my foot before wrapping it in gauze and taping it.

As he's doing it, feelings from the past come rushing forward, but I push them away as quickly as they came. This is who I fell in love with. This guy who is taking care of me and acting concerned about my wellbeing. Back then, he fooled me into thinking this is the type of man he is, but now I know better. It's all an illusion. He pretends to care and then he belittles you and hurts you. If he cared so much about me, he never would've hurt me. Physically and emotionally.

When he's finished, I push myself off the ground, and he holds a hand out for me to take.

"I'm fine," I say, swatting his hand away.

I walk back to the house, only putting pressure on my heel, not the rest of my foot.

"Amelia, wait," he states, walking beside me.

"What are you doing here, Jayden?" I curtly ask.

"I asked your mom if you were coming home for Thanksgiving, and they said you'd be here. I wanted to stop by so we could talk."

"There's nothing for us to talk about," I state, pushing past him toward the front door.

The moment I get there, my mom flings open the door to find us both standing on the front step.

"Oh, Jayden! I didn't expect to see you here. Come in!" She moves to the side so we can enter the house.

When she sees my foot, she gasps. "Amelia! What did you do to your foot? Let me see it before you bleed out everywhere," she looks toward Jayden, "please make yourself at home while I help her."

I want to cry. I just want to stand in the middle of this room, cry, and scream. I don't want Jayden here. I don't want to be here. I want to be back in New York with Bash. I should've gone to Thanksgiving with him and his family.

As much as I want to throw Jayden out and tell my mom off, I don't. I let her lead me to the bathroom as she helps get my foot to stop bleeding. It bled through the wrap he had already put on it. I let her berate me for going outside without shoes on. I let her tell me how I should talk with him and listen to what he has to say. I just let it all happen.

Jayden joined us for our Thanksgiving meal, which makes me believe my mom basically invited him. I was wondering why she was cooking so much food for just the three of us. Now I see why. She still acts like she had nothing to do with him showing up today. We all know that's a lie.

My dad mostly stayed to himself until it was time to eat. I tried to pretend everything was okay with the world. I talked about my new job in New York, but left out any mention of Bash. My mom didn't bring him up either, which I think means she's thankful I didn't with Jayden here. She wants me to get back together with him, and I don't understand why.

Jayden left shortly after eating, which confused the shit out of me. Why the hell did he come here if he wasn't going to try to talk me into getting back together with him? He didn't even contact me that night or the next morning. I'm so confused, but thankful.

As I carry my luggage down the stairs, my mom stops me. "Your father and I have somewhere to be, so I hope you don't mind, but I asked Jayden to bring you to the airport."

My heart stops. My heart literally stops in my chest. I feel it skip those few beats before it comes back and tries to break out of my ribcage.

"I'll get an Uber," I state.

"Nonsense! He's already in the driveway waiting for you," she says, giving me a hug.

She's serious. I don't even know what to say right now, never mind what I should do. What I should do is ignore Jayden and walk straight into an Uber, but we know I'm not going to. I'm going to do what my mom asked me to do because that's who I am. Always trying to please her, even when it's against my best interest.

"Alright. Where's dad?" I ask, so I can say goodbye.

He walks around the corner and pulls me into a hug. "It was good seeing you, Amelia. We'll have to come to New York and see your place soon."

I nod and hug him back. We finish our goodbyes before I walk out the front door with my suitcase. Jayden exits the car and grabs it from me, throwing it in the trunk. I get in the car before he can pretend to be a gentleman and open the door for me. Not that he did when we were dating, but he's clearly trying to impress my parents and me by pulling all these cards.

I try to be as polite as possible, so I don't set him off. I know even the littlest movement or saying will do that. "Thank you for the ride to the airport."

He gives me what looks like a genuine smile. "You're welcome. I'm glad I could because we need to talk."

I stare out the window so I don't have to face him. I know where this is going, and I know that I need to do my best to stay calm. I'm anything but calm.

"Amelia... I need to apologize for my behavior with you. It is unacceptable to touch you, and I have no excuse. I'm asking for your forgiveness, and I want to move forward. I'm even seeing a therapist to help me," he states.

My head snaps toward him. "Really?"

He nods. "Yeah. I told you, it's unacceptable. I love you, Amelia. I'll do whatever it takes to get you back."

I look out the window again to keep myself calm before saying, "What about the girl you were cheating on me with?"

"She's nothing. I haven't spoken to her since you left. I didn't realize how stupid I was being until you left me. I need you back, Amelia."

My heart is racing again. This is where it gets tricky. I want nothing to do with him anymore, and I wish I could just tell him that, but I can't. He could snap at anything I say or even any expression I give him.

"I appreciate you saying that," I state.

"So, you'll give us another chance?" he asks.

"I need a little time to think about it, if that's okay?" I ask, but only because I want him to feel like he's in control and making the decision.

He thinks for a moment. "Of course."

We don't speak for the rest of the ride to the airport. Instead of pulling up to drop me off, he pulls into the cell phone lot. I feel nauseous not knowing what's coming but knowing at the same time.

He parks the car. "Did you have enough time to think?"

I shake my head no.

His face becomes angry. Shit. See! Why am I so stupid? What do I do? Should I just say yes, that I just need to get things wrapped up back home? It would be easy to get out of this situation, but then what happens when he comes after me there? He'd be even more angry that I lied to him and led him on.

"Amelia, I don't think you understand," he states angrily.

"What?" I ask with a shaky voice.

"You are mine. You're going to come back to me because I'm not done with you yet, especially since you now have a CEO in your pocket."

My back stiffens at his words. "How do you... Never mind, I'm not coming back to you Jayden. We're over."

I quickly try to exit the car, but he grabs my arm and pulls me toward him. His grip tightens, and it hurts. He's holding my arm so tightly I'm afraid a bone is going to snap.

He leans in my face and spit hits me when he says, "I don't think I've made myself clear. You will be coming back to me. You have two weeks to make your preparations, or I'll drag you back myself, but first, you need to get all the money you can out of your rich boyfriend."

"I don't have a boyfriend," I state as sincerely as I can.

"That's a lie. If you didn't, then your stuff wouldn't be in New York right now. His men paid me a visit and demanded I send him all your things. He was at least kind enough to pay me to do it," he says, laughing.

What? Bash did that? I shake my head. I can't think about this right now. I need to concentrate on what's happening and how he's gripping my arm so I can't leave. As scared as I am, I know I need to fight back. I need him to know that I'm not coming back to him, no matter his threats.

"No," I state, trying to keep my voice even.

It happens out of nowhere. I don't see it coming until my head is slammed against the dashboard. Pain radiates from the bottom of my eye to the top of my head. He grabbed my hair and slammed my head into it twice. When he lifts my head back up, I hold my hand to my right eye, trying to keep my composure, but needing to get out of here.

My fight-or-flight instinct is appearing again, and I need to leave. I push him away from me and thankfully he lets go of my arm. Grabbing my purse, I race out of the car through the parking lot. I don't even care about the distance to the terminal. I jog the whole way there, not looking back, and leaving my luggage in his trunk.

CHAPTER TWENTY-SEVEN

BASH

I had a great Thanksgiving with my friends and family, but I missed Amelia like crazy. I couldn't stop thinking about her and wishing she was there with us. She and Everly would really get along.

Everly is a lot of fun, especially when we're all together. Everything went smoothly and there wasn't any drama, though Jake's prank could have caused one. Whenever Everly and Jake are together during a holiday, they always play a prank. I wasn't sure if that would continue this year, but it did.

When Mrs. Crawford stated her cook apologized for leaving the buns in the oven versus serving them, Jake took the opportunity to play his prank. He stood next to Everly and started his announcement with, "Well, since we're talking about buns in the oven..." Then proceeded with, "Everly and I have some news..."

Needless to say, we all thought he knocked her up, which created a lot of tension in the room. The way he continued talking verified all our assumptions. I think Jake would've gone on longer with the prank if Mr. Monroe, Everly's father, hadn't spoken up. Jake pretended like he had no idea why anyone would have come to that conclusion and then continued to tell us all about a charity they were starting together to help mothers and their babies. Once we found out he hadn't knocked her up, we were all happy for their charity. I was thankful James didn't kill him anyway. They seem to have worked out their differences and are sticking with it. I held James' arm while Jake was speaking, just in case.

Hank also has a lead on the guy that has been hacking Tim and my systems. Or I should say, woman. I'm not sure how, but he found out it's a woman and that it's not a coincidence both Tim and I are getting hit by her. It may be a bit before we actually catch her, but I'm confident Hank will get the job done.

I spot Amelia heading out of the airport, and my happiness quickly fades when I see her face. She looks exhausted, but that's not what concerns me. Her right eye is swollen and bruised, with a cut above her eyebrow.

Wells and I race to meet her. I grab her face, inspecting it further as she tries to push me away.

"What happened?" I ask, trying to keep my cool.

She grabs my wrists and forces me to let her go. "I fell... It's fine."

She's lying. Wells and I glance at each other with knowing looks. I'm not going to push her out here in public, so I go to grab her luggage and realize she doesn't have it with her.

"Where's your suitcase?" I ask.

She sighs. "I lost it. Can we... go?"

She looks defeated, so I drop it and lead her to the car. Once we get on the road, I break the silence. I know she's lying, and I know she doesn't want to talk about it. I need her to.

Resting my hand on her knee, I scoot closer to her. "Amelia, I need you to tell me what happened."

Tears streak down her cheeks, and she shakes her head. Shit, did someone do this to her? Did she get mugged or worse? I shake my head, trying not to come up with scenarios when it could have been something as simple as falling and losing her luggage. It wouldn't be farfetched with her.

"Please, tell me," I say softly.

"You have to promise you won't do anything or tell anyone," she whispers.

She may be whispering, but I know Wells can hear her. We make eye contact in the rearview mirror.

"Both of you," she states seriously toward Wells.

I nod, and he does as well. I don't know what she's about to tell me, but I have a feeling this is a promise I'm going to break. I never want to lie to her or break her trust, but I will do whatever it takes to keep her safe and happy.

"My ex showed up yesterday at my parents' for Thanksgiving. I don't know if they invited him or what, but he ate with us and then left..." she pauses and looks out the window.

Anger rises. "Why didn't you tell me?"

We talked on the phone for a little last night, and she didn't mention any of this. I never would've guessed anything was wrong. Maybe I was too caught up in my own good day that I couldn't see it.

"I didn't think anything would come of it. I didn't hear from him again until he showed up to bring me to the airport," she continues.

She places her head on my shoulder and doesn't say anything more. I'm going to have to ask it, but I already know the answer.

"Did he do this to you?" I swallow the lump in my throat.

She doesn't answer aloud, but I feel her nod against my shoulder. Fuck! He's dead. The bastard is a dead man.

"I'm going to kill him," I breathe through clenched teeth.

Amelia sits up straight. "No!"

"Amelia..." I try to rein in my temper.

"No, you promised. He's not worth it. I told him we're over and he was just mad. I'm safe in New York. There's no way he'd come out here or even be able to find me," I say.

If her parents allowed him to share Thanksgiving with them, then I have no doubt they'll share her address with him. Clearly, they don't know what he's done to her or else they wouldn't have invited him. Right?

"Do your parents know?" I ask.

"No. I haven't told them."

"Why?"

She sighs. "It's embarrassing, okay?"

Seriously? She hasn't told anyone because it's embarrassing?

I shake my head. "It's not embarrassing, at least not for you. It should be for him to treat any woman like this. Amelia, if you won't let me take care of it for you, then you need to go to the police."

"I can't," she says.

"Why not?"

"I just can't, okay? Please, just let it go. I'm not going back to San Diego. He can't hurt me again."

I want to ask if he has her luggage, but I know the answer to that. I can't believe he would do this to her. How could anyone do this to her or any woman? I gave the low life a chance to make things right and send her stuff to me. I received it a couple of days ago and haven't had the opportunity to tell her yet. I should've just had Wells kill the guy versus give him some money to do the right thing. I was hoping he'd get the hint, and that the money meant staying away from Amelia.

She's quiet the rest of the ride home, and I am too. I can't say anything because now I'm brought to the past thinking about Everly. When I found out about her being raped by her ex, I wanted to kill the man, just like I want to kill Amelia's ex. There was so much happening at that moment, I didn't know what to do, but I knew that Everly needed me, us. I wasn't there the way I wanted to be, and I'm not going to make that mistake again.

The memories of that summer at the lake house are impossible to forget.

Jake comes back into the room after being gone with Everly for over half an hour. By the way he looks, I know what he did. Shit.

Clearly, I'm not the only one that notices. Ben starts pushing Jake to tell us what he and Everly were up to, but Jake's not budging. I sigh as I feel we need to end this conversation.

After Jake just laughs and shrugs at Ben's last attempt to get it out of him, I say, "So, you did? Does that mean you won the bet?"

Since the topic isn't going to be dropped, I figured this might sound better to James than hearing how Jake fucked the girl James is in love with.

Jake doesn't even get a chance to answer before James is pushing him against the wall and growling, "Tell me you didn't!"

Jake yells, "She asked me for it! I asked her three times to make sure she wanted it."

James pulls Jake forward and slams him against the wall. This time with a punch to the face.

Anger courses through me. I know James is pissed, but he has no right to hit my brother.

We all freeze for a moment as we hear Everly yell out, "James!"

While James is distracted by Everly's presence, I take this opportunity to make my way over to them. Ben is clearly going to be on James' side, so I have my guard up with them both. James still has Jake against the wall, clutching the collar of his shirt. I get right up to him.

"Let go, James," I threaten.

James ignores me and screams in Jake's face, "Tell me you're lying Jake!"

"Then that would be a lie. She was great in bed." Jake smiles as he says it.

Fuck. My brother doesn't fight physically. He fights with words, and he just pissed James off even more.

I catch James' hand before it lands on Jake again and push him off. Jake takes this opportunity to slip away from the wall to my side.

James is furious. "Fuck you, man! She was just raped all year by her asshole boyfriend. She doesn't need this!"

I can feel the tension in the air as we all stop breathing and look toward Everly to confirm. There's no denying it. She's been fucking raped. Everly turns and runs out the front door, leaving it open behind her.

"Everly!" James and I yell out at the same time.

Jake steps forward, but I stop him. "Stay here, Jacob."

He wants to argue, but he doesn't. I think it's best if he keeps his distance from Everly and James at the moment. I quickly let one of her security guards know what happened, leaving out the details, and head out myself to look for her.

It's dark and without a flashlight, you can't see anything. I turn on mine and search the opposite direction James and Ben went. If I were her, I wouldn't be sitting out in the open. I would've taken to the woods but not gone too far in because of the darkness.

It starts raining, which calms my anger a little. I'm so mad at James right now for his reaction to Jake, but I'm also angry at Jake for taunting James. I'm pissed that bet was made in the first place. I want to kill her ex, and I have mixed emotions about Everly not telling us herself that this happened.

I find Everly curled up against a tree with her face buried in her knees, sobbing. She looks so broken, and I hate that I don't know how to help her. I hate that she didn't feel comfortable enough to come to me about what happened.

I place my hand on her shoulder, and she jumps. "Everly, let's go back."

Kneeling in front of her, I try to help her up. She refuses and pushes me away, but I don't budge.

"Leave me alone, Bash," she says weakly.

My heart drops at how weak she sounds. How did I not notice something like this going on with her? Why didn't I insist that we talk to her more during the school year? Why was I so selfish and didn't think of her much, except during the summer when she was with us? She has always been so strong. I'm an idiot.

"I'm not leaving you Everly. Let's get out of the rain and we can talk," I plead with her.

She takes a moment but finally decides to stand up. I grab her arm to help steady her. As we start walking forward, she trips, but I catch her and wrap my arm around her waist. I don't let go of her for the whole walk back. I wish there was something more I could do for her.

As we get back to the cabin, I quickly text Ben, Jake, and James, letting them know I found her. They all walk in drenched, including Jake. I see he didn't take my advice to stay back.

As she notices everyone surrounding us, including her security guards, she runs upstairs and the door slams behind her. Jake and James both move to follow her, but I hold Jake back.

"Give her some time," I say.

He shakes his head. "I'm not leaving her alone."

I interrupt, "Let James go. He's the one that shared her secret. He needs to apologize."

"So do I," he states with hurt in his eyes.

I shake my head. "No, you don't. You didn't do anything wrong."

He pulls away from me. "Yeah, I did. I let this happen to her. I should've seen something. I should've made sure she was comfortable telling me anything. I should've..."

I stop him there. "That's on all of us, Jake. We all should have."

Ben steps up beside him, placing his hand on his shoulder. "He's right. It's on us all, not just you."

Jake runs his hand through his hair and walks out the front door. It's still pouring outside, but he doesn't care. Ben and I let him go.

The next day, the four of us put our feud with each other on hold and confronted Adam. We beat him up and threatened him, but Jake did the most damage. He's rarely physical, so it shocked me, and it was the first time I realized he too was in love with Everly. Adam continued to be an issue down the line, so clearly, our attempts didn't work. I should've killed him. We should've killed him. Regardless, I won't be making the same mistake twice.

I insisted Amelia stay at my place and have a doctor see her. She refused to get checked out, so I had one come to us. He didn't think she had a concussion and would heal quickly, thankfully. I held her in bed until she fell asleep, then I met with Wells in the living room.

"Let me take care of it," he states before I can get a word out.

"No," I say, knowing he knows what I'm going to do.

He shakes his head. "You are not a killer."

"I will be whoever she needs me to be. Right now, she needs him gone, forever," I say, brushing past him.

He grabs my arm to stop me. "I won't let you go."

"How are you going to stop me? I'm not letting him go. I've fucked up once. I'm not going to fuck up again."

His eyes soften. "That wasn't your fault, and neither is this. I'm going to take care of it. If you don't like the outcome, we'll do it your way."

"You'll let me kill him?" I ask, making sure I understand what he's saying.

"If it comes down to that, yes. If you think that's the only way, then I'll hand you the gun and help you pull the trigger," he states seriously.

Fuck. Wells is a good guy, and I know he has my best interest in mind. He cares about me, and he's got my back no matter what. He deserves my trust.

I sigh and he lets go of my arm. "Alright. We'll do it your way. Keep me updated."

He nods and leaves my apartment. I do trust him, but I'm just afraid whatever he's going to do isn't enough. What if it's like the situation with Everly, and he comes back to hurt her again? I wouldn't be able to forgive myself. I pace the room for a moment and decide it's okay. I'm going to see what Wells does, and if I think there's any chance he can hurt her again, I'll take him out myself with Wells by my side.

Chapter Twenty-Eight

AMELIA

I left Bash's apartment the next morning because I needed to figure out what to do about Jayden and how to keep Bash safe. Now that Jayden knows about him, I'm not sure what he'll do. I also haven't brought up the fact that I know Bash has my stuff. He also hasn't mentioned it. I promised that I would talk to him the next day. It's the next day, and I'm dreading the conversation.

I pull out my phone and stare at the screen. How am I going to tell him that I just need a little time? We aren't officially back together yet, and here I am asking for some distance. It's not what I want, but it's what's best. Jayden told me he would come for me in two weeks, and I can't have Bash anywhere near me. I need to cut him off here and now, so there's no chance he'll be around when Jayden decides to show up.

I blow out the breath I was holding and press the call button by his name.

"Hey," Bash answers hesitantly.

"Hey," I respond.

"How are you?" he asks.

"I'm okay..."

There's an awkward silence, and I don't know what to say, even though I've rehearsed it fifty times before calling him. My heart is beating so fast I think I might have a heart attack.

"Amelia, I..." Bash says at the same time I say, "Bash, I..."

He chuckles. "Go ahead."

I close my eyes and wish I didn't have to say this. "Look, Bash. I appreciate everything you've done for me, and I really wish things were different, but right now..."

Bash tries to interrupt me. "Amelia, stop."

"No," I interrupt back. "I need to say this. I told you I'm not in a position to have a relationship, and that still stands. I'm sorry if I led you on, but right now, I need to concentrate on myself and figure things out. It's best if we don't see or talk to each other anymore."

I hang up the phone before he can say anything else. It rings immediately with him calling, but I ignore it and toss my phone to the end of my bed. I head to the bathroom and turn the shower on, hoping it'll help me feel better about what I just did. I'm an idiot, I know. Bash was the best thing that's ever happened to me, and I love him. I fucking love him, and I just told him I don't want to be with him anymore. My life is a soap opera, and it's getting ridiculous.

I step into the shower and let the water run over me. This is for the best. Without him as a distraction, I can figure out what to do about Jayden.

"It's the weekend, I promise he won't be there," Sierra says, looking at me with her puppy dog eyes.

I sigh. "Fine, as long as you're quick."

She smiles. "I promise!"

I roll my eyes as I follow her into the building that I no longer work in. Sierra convinced me to spend a little time with her today, and I figured it would help get my mind off Bash. Of course, she would forget some important documents at work and have to go retrieve them on our way to hang out.

We make it up to her office, and she throws a pile of papers in my arms.

"Go make copies of these real quick," she says as she continues shifting through her files.

"Seriously? I'm not your assistant anymore," I state.

She rolls her eyes. "No, but you're my best friend. If you want to get out of here as quick as possible, then you'll go make those copies."

Sighing, I respond, "Alright, fine."

As I'm about to walk out the door, she yells, "Wait! I forgot this copy machine is broken, so you'll have to go a floor down to use theirs."

Of course it is. I reposition the files in my arms to ensure they don't fall everywhere as I head into the elevator. I get to the next floor down and make the copies in just under five minutes. As I'm entering the elevator to go back up, I almost drop the copies but quickly flatten them against my side. A loud thud on the elevator floor catches my attention, as I watch my phone bounce three times before falling directly into the crack of the elevator, creating a soft thud way down below.

My breath catches as I stare at the crack... and stare at the crack... and continue staring at the crack, completely frozen. That. Did. Not. Just. Happen.

How many times have I stared at the crack of an elevator floor and thought "what would happen if my phone fell down there?" Well, now I know what would happen... I'd cry, scream, and panic. Why did that have to happen? Was it not secure enough in my jacket pocket? How did it bounce just right to go down there?!

I exit the elevator on the same floor I made the copies. It's fine. It'll be fine. I'll just call Joe, the maintenance guy, who always works on the weekends. I go to fish my phone out of my jacket pocket, then facepalm myself after realizing... MY PHONE FELL DOWN THE ELEVATOR CRACK. Fuck me.

Placing the papers down on a random desk, I pick up the desk phone and dial maintenance. Joe picks up on the third ring.

"Maintenance, this is Joe."

"Hey Joe! It's Amelia!" I state cheerfully.

"Oh, Amelia! What are you doing here?" he asks.

"Well... I didn't come here to drop my phone down the elevator crack... but that's what I did."

There's a long pause on the phone.

"I'll be up in a few," he says, hanging up the phone.

Ah, good old Joe. He's not the least bit surprised at what I just told him. In fact, I think he'd have been disappointed if I hadn't done something stupid.

I make my way back to Sierra's office and place the files on her desk. She finishes typing something on her computer, then stands, grabbing her keys.

"Thanks! Ready?" she asks.

I squint my eyes at her. "Well, I would be, if I wasn't waiting for Joe."

She looks at me confused. "Why are you waiting for Joe?"

I shrug my shoulders. "I don't know... I might have dropped my phone down the elevator crack."

She stares at me. "You... Okay, cool."

Yeah, she has no idea what to say to that. She's not surprised, at least, that's for sure. Sierra and I spend some time relaxing in her office while waiting for Joe to show up with my phone. At least, I'm hoping he's going to show up with my phone.

We hear the elevator doors open, so we meet Joe halfway in the hall.

"I have some good news and bad news," Joe says.

"Of course," I state.

He hands me my phone. "Good news is I found your phone. Bad news is it's toast."

He's right. Not only is the screen completely cracked, but the phone refuses to turn on. Great. I just got this phone. Thankfully, I got the accidental warranty on it after my previous phone mishap.

"Thanks Joe. I appreciate you retrieving it for me," I say sincerely.

"Anytime... but you know, if you wanted to see me, you could've just stopped by or called."

I laugh. "Oh, now you tell me. Alright, I'll do that next time."

Joe gives me a hug. "It's good to see you Amelia. We miss you around here."

"Oh, I'm sure you do. It must get boring without me," I say, giving him a hug back.

"Don't be a stranger. Come visit," he says while getting on the elevator.

My heart sinks. I would love to come visit him and some of the others. I do miss it here, but I don't know if I'll ever be able to. I have a feeling Bash isn't going to be as forgiving this time for me walking away.

Chapter Twenty-Nine

AMELIA

Several days have gone by since I officially told Bash we're over. Everything I left behind in San Diego was sent to my apartment. Every single one of my books, clothes, blankets, towels, and small trinkets are all here. The person delivering the boxes handed me a note from Bash. It explained how he got Jayden to send my stuff to him a little bit ago and it was time that I got it all back. It also stated that he is waiting for me.

He tried calling and texting me for a few days, but he finally gave up. He hasn't tried to contact me for a full twenty-four hours. That's the longest he has gone without reaching out to me. I try not to let it hurt, but it does. It's exactly what I asked for, so I shouldn't be upset.

I lay here awake, just like I have been the past few nights. I can't sleep anymore, and everyone notices. My coworkers are worried about me, and even my students have made comments about how tired I look. The kicker to all of this is that I still haven't figured out what I'm going to do about Jayden when he shows up here like he promised. I keep saying I have more time to figure it out, but eventually, time is going to run out.

I squint at my phone as it rings at this early morning hour. It's an unknown number, but I have a feeling I should pick it up. Who would be calling me at this time?

"Hello?" I answer.

"Amelia, it's Jake."

I freeze. Why would Jake be calling me? How did he get my number?

"What's wrong?" I ask, knowing something has to be.

"Bash is fine. He just... I think he needs you right now," he says.

"Huh?" I ask aloud. I didn't mean to actually say that.

"He can explain things to you, but we've all had a rough night. He really needs you, Amelia. If you care about him, you'll go check on him."

What the hell is happening right now? I'm supposed to be at work in a couple of hours, but if what Jake says is true and Bash needs me, then I need to be there. I love him. I'm trying to stay away for his sake, not mine. If Jake is calling me, this is serious. How can I turn down helping Bash when he's done nothing but be there for me?

"Alright, I'll go check on him," I say, and Jake hangs up the phone.

Throwing the covers off, I toss on my clothes from yesterday. I don't have time to figure out what to wear. I don't even think as I get in my car and drive to Bash's place. When I get there, Wells is waiting for me outside.

"What's going on Wells?" I ask, out of breath.

Clearly, I was holding my breath the entire drive, or I've been running a marathon. I'm not sure.

"I'll let you in. He's had a rough night. He'll explain it to you," he says.

Why is everyone being so vague with me? Whatever, the faster I get to him, the better. My heart is racing, and I'm antsy on the elevator ride up to his apartment. Wells doesn't knock before unlocking the door and letting me in. Once I enter, he closes it behind me. Okay?

I look around, but the place is dark. It's as if he's not even here.

"Bash?" I call out, but there's no answer.

I walk toward the bedroom and call out again, "Bash?"

"Amelia?" he calls out, which sounds like he's in his office.

I make my way to his office door to find him sitting behind his desk with a glass of something alcoholic. I can smell it from here.

"What's going on?" I ask, cautiously approaching him.

He places the glass down and rubs his hands over his face. His face is red, his eyes are swollen, and his hair's a mess. Something has happened, and my heart breaks for him. Jake was wrong. Bash is not fine.

I sit on his lap and wrap my arms around him. "Tell me what happened."

"Everly almost died," he states matter-of-factly.

"What?!" I lean back to look at his face.

"She was kidnapped yesterday. I spent all night at James' place trying to help... But you know what I realized? I couldn't help. I couldn't do shit to help her. I sat there like an idiot calling in all sorts of favors from people I know, but no one could find her. I kept telling James she would be okay, but I was fucking terrified. I couldn't do anything!"

He slides me off his lap and paces the room. He went from looking sad, to emotionless, to angry in five seconds. I feel all those things though, too. Everly was kidnapped? Why? I have so many questions.

"She's okay though? She's safe?" I ask, knowing that's the most important question.

He shakes his head. "Physically, she's fine."

He looks like he's about to be angry again, so I move closer and hug him. "Let's go. Let's go take a shower and get some rest. Then we can talk, okay?"

He doesn't argue and lets me lead him to the bathroom. I get the shower started and help him get undressed. Once he's in, I grab some clothes from his closet and lay them out for him. I also send a quick text to the principal saying that I'm sick and won't be in today. They'll figure it out. Bash needs me.

When Bash gets out of the shower, I lead him to the bed and lie with him. He's quiet, and I'm hoping he falls asleep to get some rest. I want to know what happened, but I want to make sure he's taken care of first.

"Why did you leave me?" he whispers.

A lump in my throat forms. "Bash..."

"No... I need to know. Why did you leave me?"

"We don't need to talk about this right now," I say soothingly.

"Yes, we do," he says as he rolls on top of me, trapping me underneath him.

"Bash..."

"I need to know why you left. I fucking love you Amelia. I love you, and I need you..." he pauses for a moment before continuing, "but you clearly don't love me."

He rolls off, back onto the bed, facing the wall. My heart physically hurts, and I feel the tears stream down my face. He truly believes I don't love him? Of course he does. I pushed him away. I told him I didn't want to be with him.

I grab his shoulder and force him onto his back. This time, I climb on top of him and cup his face to look at me.

"I love you so much Bash. It hurts how much I love you, and it hurts to see you like this. I'm sorry. I didn't know what to do. I want to be with you, but I'm afraid of Jayden and what he could do to you. I was dumb and pushed you away... I'm... scared..."

It takes me a moment to comprehend what's happening. Bash flips me over so he's back on top and his mouth is on mine. He's frantic as he kisses me and moves his hands over my body. I close my eyes and savor every touch.

He unbuttons my shirt and pulls it off, along with my bra. His mouth finds a nipple as he sucks and plays with it. My breathing becomes erratic, and I'm pretty sure I'm about to come just from his touch. It's been so long. I have so many emotions I've been bottling up and they are all channeling into this moment,

"Bash..." I say, not wanting him to stop, but wanting to make sure this is what he needs right now.

He stops and presses his forehead against mine, panting. "I need you, Amelia."

I need him too. I grab the back of his head and my mouth crashes on his. Our tongues collide, dancing with each other with neediness. I pull his shirt off and toss it to the side, working his pants next. Once those are off, mine join his, and we continue until we're both without clothes.

He kisses down my stomach and almost reaches where I want him so badly, but I stop and pull him back up.

"What?" he asks, confused.

I push him down onto the bed and climb on top of him. I don't say anything as I do exactly what he just did to me and kiss down his stomach. I grip his erection in my hand and stroke as I watch him lie there with his eyes closed and teeth biting his bottom lip.

I take him in my mouth, and he groans, grabbing the back of my head.

"Jesus, Amelia."

I can't help but smile at his words, and I take him in deeper. I torture him slowly until I can tell he can't take it anymore. I crawl up and we waste no time as he pulls me on top of himself to ride him.

We're both a panting and sweaty mess as I ride him harder until he rolls us over to take over.

He whispers in my ear. "As much as I love you fucking me, I want to make love to you."

The moment he finishes that sentence, I come, hard. He quickly follows, kissing my neck, earlobe, and then forehead before climbing off me, rolling over on the bed.

"I didn't use a condom..." he whispers into the darkness.

My heart stops. No, he didn't.

"I'm clean," I state, as if that's what he's worried most about.

"Me too," he says.

We both stare at each other with tense expressions. I know what he's waiting to hear, and how I wish I could say those words to him.

"I'm not on the pill," I finally spit out.

He's silent as he stares at the ceiling. We both know what that could mean. Odds are I'm not ovulating. Honestly, I don't have the energy to figure out when my last period was at this moment, but I will later. I'm more concerned about what his response is going to be.

"I'm sorry. I should've been more responsible," he says, rolling onto his side to face me.

I do the same. "It's my responsibility too."

"Should I go get the Plan B pill?" he asks.

I shrug. "We can, but if we're being honest, I'll probably end up throwing it up. I've tried it before, but it made me sick."

"Then we don't need it," he states.

"Are you sure?" I ask, willing to do whatever will make him comfortable with this.

He pulls me closer to him. "Amelia, if you happen to get pregnant from tonight, I'm okay with that. I meant what I said. I love you. We'll figure it out, together."

I close my eyes and let out a sigh of relief. I needed to hear that. I don't want a baby right now, but it's nice knowing that if it happened, he wouldn't run away. It's more than I've given him. I've done nothing but run away.

"Okay," is all I get out.

He holds me tight against him, and it doesn't take long before we both fall asleep.

CHAPTER THIRTY

BASH

It's Christmas Day, and I get to spend it with Amelia. She's coming with me to celebrate with my family and friends. We celebrate every year with the Crawfords and occasionally Everly and her father. This year is the first year in a while that we'll all be together.

Amelia and I are in a much better place than we were a few weeks ago. After Everly was kidnapped, I realized I'm not letting Amelia go. She had her reservations because of her ex, but after I told her everything that happened with Everly, she agreed to not waste any more time together. That situation showed me that you never know when your last day will be. We're not going to waste it.

Everly is doing well, all things considered. When she was kidnapped, we found out she was pregnant. James didn't even know. It wasn't the best way to find out, but he's really excited to be a father. I'm happy for them. It's about time they settle down. He proposed to her last night, so I expect some grand reveal to show they are engaged when they show up today.

Speaking of pregnancy, Amelia started her period a week after we had unprotected sex. While I wouldn't have been opposed to her being pregnant, I was relieved. We need more time together before we add that to our relationship. There are still things she also needs to get used to with my lifestyle and who I am. After Everly's kidnapping, I've been more cautious with Amelia. I've had Wells trailing her, and I'm planning on hiring her own protection detail.

Amelia has been nervous about her ex coming for her. Wells has a few things in the works for him, so Jayden won't be bothering Amelia ever again. She doesn't know this yet, though. I don't want to tell her until everything is final. She's either been staying the night at my place, or I stay at hers. As much as I want her to move in with me, I know she's not ready yet.

We make it to the Crawford's house and Mrs. Crawford greets Amelia like she's royalty. She has always treated me like her own son, which I appreciate. I love the woman like a mother. I know she's excited to have another girl in the house besides Everly.

"Glad to see Amelia here," Jake says from behind me.

I turn around to find him looking awful. Okay, my brother looks great as always, but I see right through the mask he puts on. There's something bothering him, and my heart sinks at knowing what it might be.

"You doing okay, brother?" I ask, but know how he'll answer.

"Always. Did you see what the old man is wearing?" he asks, nodding toward our father.

I find him sitting at the island with Mr. Crawford and squint my eyes so I can see him better. His suit is normal, but Jake's right, he's wearing something odd. A tie. Not any tie, but a tie with Santa Claus on it.

"What bet did he lose to wear that?" I ask.

Jake laughs. "He wore it on his own. Don't mention it though. He'll bite your head off."

I laugh because I know that's true. My father has been acting odd lately, and this confirms it. There's definitely something going on with him too, but we both know he'll never tell us if we ask.

"Come on, let's get a drink," Jake says, leading me toward the kitchen.

Shortly after getting settled and watching Amelia interact with Mrs. Crawford and my mom, James and Everly arrive.

Just like I expected, Everly has a ring on her finger. Everyone crowds them, congratulating them. I stay back and wait until the crowd dies before heading over to James. Everly has already made her way to Amelia. I know they're going to become good friends.

"Is that your girlfriend?" James asks, looking toward the girls.

"It is, that's Amelia," I state, as if he doesn't know her name by now.

"You love her." It's not a question.

I nod. "I never understood how you could be so sure about you and Everly, but I get it now. She's it for me. We've only known each other for half a year, but I know she's it."

He pats me on the shoulder. "I'm glad you worked it out with her. Now come introduce us."

We walk toward the girls, and I introduce Amelia to James. She hugs him while I give Everly a hug. I know I hold on to her a little longer than necessary, but it's just so good to see her when I thought I might never see her again.

Amelia and James start immediately talking about some tech thing, which I note. I didn't realize that Amelia was so into technology. Everly pulls me over to the side, away from everyone else.

"How are you doing?" I ask, rubbing her shoulders.

She gives me a small smile. "I'm actually doing okay."

"Good."

"I wanted to ask you about Jake," she says seriously.

"What about him?"

"Is he okay? I didn't want to say anything to him, but he doesn't look like himself lately. I mean, he acts like himself, but he just looks... sad."

I'm not surprised that she noticed too. Everly may be a rich only child, but she's actually not selfish. She can be with some things, but she loves us like brothers. She really cares about Jake.

"Yeah, I've noticed too. He doesn't want to talk about it," I say.

She nods. "Do you have any guesses on what's bothering him?"

I shake my head. I'm not about to be telling her that I think it's because of her. That he still loves her. He denies it, but I have a feeling that's at least part of it.

"Okay. Just keep an eye on him, okay?"

"Always," I say.

The rest of the night is filled with laughter and a lot of fun. I always enjoy getting together with everyone, but this year is different. It's nice having Amelia here with me. We've been glancing at each other across the room all night. When we're near each other, we're always touching, and I'm giving her quick kisses. It feels so natural having her here. The best part is, she and Everly seemed to have hit it off. Especially after the white elephant gift exchange we did. They found out they both are obsessed with Taylor Swift.

My parents make their exit, and I take the opportunity for us to sneak out. The moment we get into my apartment, I pull her in for a kiss. She moans in my mouth, and I part from her before things get too serious. I need to talk to her first.

She stares at me, wiping something from my forehead, laughing.

"What?" I ask, smiling because she's so cute.

"You have glitter on your forehead," she says while continuing to wipe at it.

I run my hands through her hair. "You have glitter all in your hair."

"I swear it multiplies and jumps," she says, giggling.

She did have a couple of drinks tonight, but she's only tipsy. She's cute when she's tipsy. We wipe a few more pieces of glitter off each other, but I don't think it's going anywhere anytime soon. Jake's white elephant gift included an exploding glitter bomb, which James got the brunt of. Good luck to the Crawfords cleaning that up.

"You ready to head to bed?" Amelia asks seductively.

"Are you tired?" I ask, knowing that's not what she means.

"I will be after some time with you." She pulls me toward the bedroom.

I laugh. "Okay, but I really need to talk to you about something first."

She freezes and concern etches her face. I didn't mean to scare her, but I really need to talk to her. I don't like keeping secrets, and I don't know how she's going to react to what I'm about to tell her.

"What is it?"

"Let's sit, first." I lead her to the couch only a few feet away.

She's quiet, waiting for me to drop the bomb. I don't know why I'm so nervous. I just don't want to lose her.

"Just rip the band-aid off Bash."

I clear my throat. "I've been doing some thinking and talking to Wells... After everything that happened to Everly, it has made me think about your safety. I've had Wells following you to make sure you're safe when you're not with me, but I was thinking about hiring someone more permanent to watch out for you when I'm not around..."

She stares at me as she processes what I said. "You've had Wells following me?"

"Just when we're not together, he's just been around when you're heading to work and home," I say, trying to think of what more I can say.

She surprises me by saying, "Okay."

"Okay?" I ask.

"Yeah, okay. If it makes you feel better to have someone looking out for me, okay. It'll take me some time to get used to, but I don't want you worrying about me," she says sincerely.

I pull her into me and kiss the top of her head. "Thank you."

She looks up at me and laughs.

"What?"

She wipes my lips with her finger. "You have glitter on your mouth."

I laugh and push her down on the couch, tickling her and attacking her with more kisses. She laughs and rolls over to the floor to escape me.

"If we're done with this conversation, I'm ready to go to bed," she says, yawning.

I cock my eyebrow at her. "Oh yeah?"

She squeals as I scoop her up into my arms and carry her into the bedroom for the night.

Chapter Thirty-One

AMELIA

Bash and I spent the rest of the year in his apartment, or more specifically, in his bed. We considered going out for New Year's Eve, but ultimately decided we preferred to start the new year concentrating on just us. Now that it's New Year's Day, we both have to concentrate on others.

I'm getting ready to head out for lunch with Sierra, and then I'll be back at my apartment for a few nights. My parents are coming to the city to visit with me. I'm surprised since they didn't seem too interested in my living here. While I start back at work tomorrow, I'll get to spend each night with them. They plan to go sightseeing during the days. Of course they are staying at my apartment, so that's why I need to be there. I'll sure miss having Bash in my bed. It's a studio apartment, so they will be sleeping on an air mattress in the living room area. Thankfully, my bedroom is sectioned off by a wall.

"Hey gorgeous." Bash comes up behind me and kisses my neck.

I turn around to kiss him. "Hey handsome."

I look him over to see him dressed professionally. I suppose he probably does need to get some work done, as I've kept him busy this past week.

"I'm heading into the office for a bit and then having dinner with my friend Tim," he explains.

"Aw, when do I get to meet him?" I ask, pouting.

He chuckles and kisses my forehead. "I promise soon. He's dying to meet you too."

"Yeah, alright."

"I need to tell you something before you go," he says seriously.

I don't respond and wait for him to continue.

"Wells has been keeping tabs on your ex and figuring out a plan to keep him away from you." He pauses.

"And?" I ask, completely surprised he's been doing this.

"And your ex will be in prison for a very long time."

"What? How long?" I ask hopeful.

"Wells made a few of Jayden's extracurricular activities come to light and more. Honestly, we'll make sure he never gets out," he promises.

I feel myself tearing up. "Thank you."

He leans in to kiss me. It's gentle at first, but it turns much more needy as he grabs my ass and pulls me in closer. I can't get enough of him and clearly, he feels the same way.

I pull away. "I really do have to go. I feel like a bad friend. I haven't been hanging out with Sierra much."

He gives me another quick kiss before leading me to the door. "You're not a bad friend. Have fun with Sierra and your parents. I'll call you tonight."

As I'm leaving the apartment, Bash continues quickly. "Oh, I'll have Wells on you through the weekend and he'll drive you to pick up your parents from the airport."

I nod. "Okay."

I know I told Bash that I'm okay with being followed, but it's a little weird. I only agreed to it because I know how much he was hurting when Everly was kidnapped, and that had to of messed with him. I want to do whatever I can to ease his anxiety. I really don't mind Wells, I like the guy, but I'm concerned about having someone that I don't know follow me around. I hope they are nice.

I'm five minutes late meeting Sierra at the restaurant. She already has a table, so I make my way to her. Before I can sit down, she stands up and flings herself at me. Literally. She pulls me into a hug and doesn't let me go.

"Amelia! I've missed you!"

I laugh and hug her back. "I've missed you too."

"We've gone too long without seeing each other. You're spending too much time with that man. Tell him we need a girls' night," she says, pouting and sitting back down.

"That man is your boss," I state.

"And you're my best friend. So, you have to tell him. I don't want to get fired," she jokes.

"Yeah, I doubt that would happen. He wouldn't survive without you at work," I tease.

"You're right, he wouldn't. Though I've noticed he's not in the office much lately. Do you happen to know why?"

Heat rises to my cheeks. Of course she knows we've been spending all our time together. To voice that I've been the one keeping him away from his job is not something I'm going to do. I know she's going to want some details about us, though.

Sierra and I spend a couple of hours at the restaurant talking and catching up. I told her a bit ago about what happened at Thanksgiving, but never really went into detail. I told her everything about Bash, his family and friends, and my parents. She told me about her non-existent love life. She's been on a few dates, but just hasn't found anyone that she's interested in.

After lunch, Wells drives me to the airport to pick up my parents. I sit in the passenger seat and watch him drive. Wells and I don't say much to each other, other than hello and small talk to be polite. I feel safe with him though and feel like he cares.

"Wells?" I break the silence.

"Yeah?" he glances at me and then back to the road.

"Thank you for helping with my ex-boyfriend situation. You didn't have to do that," I say quietly.

"He deserved it," he states.

"I know, but... you've been helping me and keeping me safe when I didn't even know it. I just wanted you to know that I appreciate it."

He nods. "I'll always do my best to keep you safe, Amelia. You're important to Bash, so you're important to me."

"You really care about Bash, don't you?" I ask, but I already know the answer.

He nods.

"How long have you known him?"

He thinks for a moment. "A long time. Bash is a good guy. Not many with his money, influence, and power are like that. He was raised with a good head on his shoulders."

"I can see that, which makes me wonder what he sees in me," I whisper.

Obviously, he heard the last part, even though I didn't intend for him to. "He sees that you're also a good person. You're not with him for his money or power. You care about him for who he is, and you make him a better person."

I laugh. "I think you have that mixed up. He makes me the better person."

He shakes his head. "You both do."

We're silent for a little bit before he continues. "Can I give you some advice?"

I look over at him. "Of course."

"I think what you and Bash have is special. Don't throw it away for miscommunications or differences. I can see how much you both love and care about each other, so hold on to that."

I let what he's saying sink in. He's right. I feel like most of our relationship problems have been because of misunderstandings and not being able to communicate correctly. We do love each other, and I don't want to lose him. I think we could build a great life together.

When we pull up to the airport, my parents are already waiting outside with their suitcases. We help them get everything in the car, and I introduce them to Wells. Once Wells heads back to the driver's side, mom pulls on my arm.

"Isn't he cute?" she whispers.

I laugh. "Mom!"

Dad shakes his head and enters the car. She knows that I'm with Bash, but I think until I'm married, she's always going to be trying to play matchmaker. She's not wrong though, Wells is really good looking. I'm surprised he doesn't have a wife and family. I don't know much about him, but I do know he doesn't wear a wedding band. Plus, I feel like Bash would've told me if he did.

The next few days fly by. My parents revealed the real reason they came to visit, which was to apologize for Jayden. Apparently, they heard about him going to prison and all the things he did. I was open with them about how he treated me, and they were so sorry for not seeing it, and also hurt that I didn't tell them.

Bash joined us for dinner one night so they could meet him, and my mother loved him. My dad did too, especially when they were talking business. There has always been a lot of tension between my parents and me, but I think we're in a better place after this trip. They promised to come out to visit more often, and now that Jayden is locked up in prison, I said I'd go out to visit them. Bash likes San Diego, so he said he'd love to travel with me.

If someone had told me last year that I would live in New York, have a billionaire boyfriend, love my teaching job, and have a good relationship with my parents, I would've told them they were high.

CHAPTER THIRTY-TWO

BASH

"You ready for this?" Ben asks, holding a blindfold out to me.

"No," I state seriously.

"It's going to be fun. It'll be like old times," he says.

"There is so much that could go wrong with this plan."

"Everything's going to go wrong with his plan," Jake says.

"Exactly, so why are we doing this?" I ask, looking between both of them.

Ben sighs and looks annoyed. "Because my brother is an idiot and refused to let me throw him a bachelor party. He claimed that he doesn't want one because he loves Everly and doesn't need to have a last night of fun before marriage."

"I can agree with that," I say.

Jake laughs. "Well, you're not getting out of having a bachelor party when you marry Amelia."

I roll my eyes. "I haven't even proposed yet. Okay, whatever, let's concentrate on what we're doing."

"Alright, put your masks on and let's do this," Ben says, securing his own mask.

We're dressed in black outfits with ski masks. James shouldn't be able to tell it's us, but honestly, I'm hoping he does. This is the stupidest plan Ben could've come up with, but he's the best man, so it's his choice on how to start James' bachelor party.

So, the idea is to kidnap James and bring him to our lake house. It's been a while since we've all been there together and figured we could have fun. He didn't want to have a normal bachelor party of going out drinking and hitting on other girls. Which I agree with. Now that I have Amelia, I have no desire to attend a bachelor party like that. As much as we would think Jake would thrive in that setting, I don't think that's true anymore.

The girls are going to meet us there after they have their spa day. The lake house has plenty of bedrooms that will fit us all with two to a room. The guys will all be sharing rooms and the girls sharing the other rooms. I know that James and Everly would prefer to be together, but we had to make this a little like a bachelor party where they don't spend the night together. Especially since I'm sure they will be spending the night together before the wedding next Friday.

Thankfully, for me, Amelia will also be there. Everly and Amelia have really hit it off. Plus, it helped that the bridal parties were uneven. Ben is James' best man while Jake and I are his groomsmen. Ashley is Everly's maid of honor, while Paige and Amelia are her bridesmaids. Amelia wasn't super comfortable being a bridesmaid when she barely knows Everly, but Everly has made a point to really get to know her.

"One..." Ben says, pulling me out of my thoughts.

"Two..." Jake says.

"Three," I state.

Ben knocks on the door while Jake and I stand to the side unseen. It only takes a few seconds before James opens the door. Ben and Jake immediately lunge at him, holding him while I tie the mask around his eyes.

"What the fuck?!" James yells and tries to force the two off him.

After getting it tied, Ben and Jake have James lifted as the three of us carry him toward the elevator.

"Fuck! Ryder!" he screams and thrashes.

I dig in my pocket for the gag. I stick it in his mouth and tie that too, hoping that'll help keep him from screaming. I was hoping not to have to use it and that he'd realize it was us by now. We did too good of a job.

While he's kicking and trying to get out of it, I'm standing in the corner of the elevator. I give it four seconds before some-one's on their knees...

"Ow! Fuck!" Jake groans, falling to his knees, grabbing his balls.

I cringe and watch the scene continue to unfold when Ben gets a knee to his stomach.

"Ugh!" Ben groans.

I laugh and continue to make myself as small as I can in the corner. I told them this wouldn't end well.

"What the fuck? Ben?!" James asks after getting the gag out of his mouth and untying his blindfold.

I take my mask off so he can see it's me, and I'm not a threat.

When the elevator door opens, Ryder is standing outside, watching the scene unfold. I can only imagine how this looks. I'm dying of laughter on the floor while both Ben and Jake are writhing in pain. James' hair is messed up, and he looks confused.

"Was that everything you were hoping for?" Ryder asks with a smirk on his face.

Ben glares at him, and Jake clears his throat, trying to stand up.

"I mean, I told them this wouldn't end well," I say, shrugging my shoulders.

"Would someone please tell me what the fuck is going on?"

"Since you didn't want a bachelor party, Ben thought it would be a good idea to kidnap you for one," Ryder says.

"And you let this happen?" James asks with concern on his face.

He shrugs his shoulders. "I wanted to watch it play out."

James shakes his head, and I walk off the elevator.

"Alright, let's go," I say as we all head to the car.

When everyone's adrenaline and pain wear off, we finally relax and tell James where we are heading. We didn't tell him exactly what's planned though.

"You guys realize that my fiancé was kidnapped recently, right?" he asks seriously.

Ben shrugs. "And that's why we made her and everyone else aware of this kidnapping."

"I'm a little disappointed James," Ryder says as he drives.

"Why?" James asks.

"You really think we haven't been keeping tabs on everything 24/7? There's no way anyone would be getting up to your apartment like that. And here you thought you were really being kidnapped." Ryder shakes his head.

"Yeah, I honestly thought you'd figure it out immediately," I say.

James shrugs. "Maybe I did and wanted an excuse to kick Jake in the balls."

Alright, that's not entirely out of the realm of possibilities. James and Jake have had many years of bad blood between them, so kicking him in the balls would probably be therapeutic.

"Eh, I deserve it," Jake says.

We all turn to stare at him, but none of us respond to that. Jake's looking out the window, deep in thought, while the rest of us give knowing looks. Yeah, this is not the time to dig into that.

After getting to the cabin, we get settled in and start a fire in the fireplace. It's freezing outside with snow on the ground and the lake icing over. It's beautiful, but it'll give us limited things to do.

I pull some beers out of the fridge and pass them around to the guys. James shakes his head, denying one.

"Really?" I ask.

"Nah. With Everly being pregnant, I'm not drinking since she can't," he states.

"Or eating queso. He's being a sap and says it's not fair he can have those things when she can't," Ben chimes in.

I cock my eyebrow. "Since when?"

"Last month. Everly had an emotional moment, so I figured I'd give it up for now," James answers.

I want to mock him, but I hold back. Honestly, if Amelia was pregnant and upset she couldn't have something, I would probably do the same thing. Growing up and falling in love is weird. We do things we never thought we would or things we used to make fun of others for.

"So, what are the plans?" James asks.

"Next on the list is something we haven't done since we were kids," Ben says excitedly.

Jake, James, and I look at each other, a little concerned. With Ben planning this, it could be anything.

"Care to elaborate?" I ask.

"Jake and me against you and James... Snowball fight!" Ben yells.

My smile grows. "You're on!"

Our snowball fights aren't normal snowball fights. We spend hours building walls and forts to protect ourselves. We create as many snowballs as possible to arm ourselves with. Ever since we were little, we'd always team up like this. James and I would take it easy on Ben and Jake, but now... Now we can unleash everything we have on them.

CHAPTER THIRTY-THREE

AMELIA

This is the best day ever. Seriously, I feel like royalty. If marrying Bash is going to mean I get this treatment whenever I want, I'm never giving him up. They say money can't buy you happiness. I might have to disagree with that. I'm pretty happy right now.

"I think I was wrong, Amelia," Paige says next to me.

We're both laying on our stomachs getting a massage. The best massage I've ever had in my life.

"About what?" I ask, sighing as the masseuse pushes all the tension out of my shoulders.

"I said I didn't want a guy with money and tried to avoid Jake. I should've given him a shot." She groans.

I laugh. "Don't you have a boyfriend?"

She sighs. "Yeah. We have a complicated relationship."

"I understand that all too well."

I'm thankful Bash and I have figured our crap out for the most part. The beginning of our relationship was rough, and

I'm pretty sure it was mostly me. I'm lucky to have him and that he stuck by me even when I was pushing him away.

"So, are you interested in Jake?" I ask.

Bash seems to think that Jake is still hung up on Everly. I honestly don't see it. I don't spend that much time with Jake, but what's bothering him doesn't seem like it's specifically Everly. Whatever, it's not my place, but if we can get him a girlfriend, maybe he'd be happy.

"Nah. I really like Matteo. I mean, did I used to fantasize about that hot man? Of course," she giggles.

I laugh. "Uh yeah. He looks just like Bash, so I get it. And if he's even half as good as Bash is..."

I stop myself and now I'm blushing. What am I doing? I don't talk to others about my sex life. I especially don't in front of strangers.

"Are you guys talking about Bash and Jake?" Everly shouts over to us.

How on earth did she hear us?

"No!" Both Paige and I yell out at the same time.

We all laugh because it's so obvious we are.

The ninety-minute massage ends too soon, but we're not done. We spend another two hours getting mani pedis with gel polish, so they last until the wedding next Friday. My feet and hands have never felt so soft in my life.

It didn't stop there. We also got our hair done. Like full wash, cut, and highlights. After they blew out my hair and curled it, I look like a different person. Oh, and we got facials. It was a full day spa treatment that I didn't know I needed. Again, if I can get this once a month, I think I'll be the happiest person on the planet.

"Do you do this often?" I ask Everly.

She laughs. "No, not really. I'm rethinking that now."

"We should do it a few times a year together. Especially after you have the baby. You're going to deserve to be treated like a queen," I say.

I'm really excited for her to have the baby. I know we haven't known each other for long, but she's really nice and fun to hang out with. I thought she would be snobby, but she's down to earth and doesn't judge me.

"I'd like that," she replies.

After we're all relaxed and glammed up, we head to the lake house to meet the boys. I haven't heard from Bash all day, so it makes me curious what they've been up to. It's a bachelor party, so I pictured them going out to a bar or strip club before heading there for the night. My stomach turns just thinking about it. I'm not usually a jealous person, but thinking about Bash looking at other women makes me queasy.

"What's wrong?" Ashley asks.

Everyone looks at me. Oops. I guess I couldn't keep the emotions off my face.

"Nothing," I state too quickly.

"You can tell us anything. We don't judge," Paige says.

I know they won't, but it feels weird telling them about my insecurities. What does it hurt, though? I can't be the only one who would feel like that.

I shrug. "I was just wondering what they've been up to all day. Did they go to a bar? A strip club?"

Everly gives me a reassuring smile before saying, "I can guarantee you they did neither."

I sigh with relief. "Do you know what they did?"

She shrugs. "I have no idea, but James isn't drinking right now because I can't. He also has no desire to look at any other woman. Bash wouldn't want to either."

I nod. "You're right."

"I'm sure they are doing something stupid at the lake house. I mean, they planned to start the day off with kidnapping James," Ashley says, laughing.

"Wait, what?" I laugh with her.

Everly nods. "Ben told me they were going to kidnap him from the apartment and drag him to the lake house. I'm curious how that went down."

Me too. That doesn't sound like a good idea, honestly. Everly was recently kidnapped for real... Oh well, I'm sure they are fine. As the girls continue talking, I watch the two men in the front seat. We're in a van, so we can all fit with Everly's two security guards in the front.

I wonder what Everly thinks about having them around all the time. I'm sure she's thankful now after what happened, but before that. Did she think it's weird? Did she resent it because she didn't have any privacy? Bash said he just hired someone, and he'd start after the wedding. I'm a little nervous.

"You get used to it," Everly states.

"Huh?" I question, looking toward her.

"Having someone around all the time. You get used to it. They become family," she continues.

"How did you know that's what I was thinking about?" I ask.

She laughs. "You were staring at them, and I know what it's like. I felt like no one trusted me and that's why I was assigned a guard at all times, but that's not the case. It's just proof of how much I'm loved."

She's right. Bash wants to have someone on me because he loves me and wants me protected. It's not that he doesn't trust me or think I can't take care of myself. He just wants to keep me safe.

"Thanks," I say.

"Anytime. Sometimes this life isn't easy or can get overwhelming, so if you ever need to talk, I'm here," she says.

"You're a really good friend, Everly," I state sincerely.

Just as we finish that conversation, we pull up to the cabin to find something we never would have expected. The guys are throwing snowballs at each other in front of the cabin. There are really tall walls of snow they are hiding behind while peeking around and throwing them. We laugh, watching as they yell at each other and are very serious. Is this really how they spent James' bachelor party?

I can't help the smile that stays on my face as I watch them. I know Bash and I are just at the beginning of our relationship, but I hope that one day I'll be marrying him. I want a family like this. I want a family where we can have fun while everyone has each other's backs. This is true happiness. So, I was wrong. They're right. Money can't buy happiness.

Chapter Thirty-Four

BASH

Watching your best friend get married with the women you love by your side is everything. James and Everly finally got married this morning, on Valentine's Day. Everly walked down the aisle as a beautiful bride. Her long dress was flowy at the bottom, but fitted the waist up, which showed the little baby bump that she has. The dress was long sleeves, and it was lacy and glittery all over. It was perfect for her.

James teared up as she came down the aisle and her father passed her off to him. Her dad gave James a hug and patted him on the shoulder. Jake and Ben were smiling widely while I was a fucking sap crying. Amelia caught me, which made her tear up.

Amelia was gorgeous standing there with her little bouquet of flowers and long purple dress. The sleeves were lacy, which matched Everly's dress. The ceremony was outdoors, so it was snowy and perfect. Thankfully, there were heaters everywhere, keeping us all warm. I couldn't imagine how cold the girls would have been otherwise.

After an hour of taking pictures, we're all at the reception primed for lunch. I'm ready to enjoy dancing with Amelia, but I notice Jake at the bar getting his third drink this morning. Amelia's with Everly and the other girls, but I catch her attention. Amelia notices my gaze and nods like she's giving me permission to be with my brother.

"Hey," I say, sitting next to him at the bar.

"Hey! This is the perfect wedding for them, isn't it?" Jake states a little too excitedly.

"It is. Happy birthday, man," I say, patting him on the shoulder. With everything going on this morning, I haven't had a chance to say it to him.

He raises his glass to me. "Thanks. Another year older..." his words drift off to a whisper as he takes a sip of his drink, "and still a fuckup."

My eyebrows squeeze together as I stare at him. "You're not a fuckup Jake."

He shrugs and slams his empty glass on the bar. "Enough! We're celebrating our best friends getting married. Let's go!"

Jake jumps off his stool and makes his way to Everly. Before I even get there, she's laughing at something he said. I push my worries aside because, obviously, he doesn't want to talk about it. Amelia comes up next to me, sliding her arm through mine.

"So, how bad was the ceremony?" she asks.

"Huh?" I question.

She slaps my shoulder. "What do you mean, huh? Were you not there during that whole incident?"

I laugh at the memory. Oh, I was there. I don't think it was as bad as she thought it was, though.

"I honestly forgot, so I don't think anyone else remembers either," I state, shrugging my shoulders.

"Oh yeah, okay. I'm sure there is absolutely no photo or video evidence either," she mocks.

Okay, so the ceremony wasn't exactly perfect. I don't know whose bright idea it was to use unity candles during it, but they did. Everly is known to not be good around fire. We've established that. James is the only one she hasn't caught on fire. At least, he was until today.

When they were lighting the unity candle, Everly accidentally caught James' sleeve on fire. He put it out quickly himself, but it startled Everly, so her candle also caught her veil on fire. Ashley was able to stomp it out. It all happened in under thirty seconds, and everything turned out fine.

Though, when Amelia stepped forward to help, she somehow stepped right off the platform they were all standing on. She rolled down the hill in the snow and was covered. I was going to jump down to help her, but Ryder, James' security, was there to help her up before I could. She was really embarrassed but was a champ pretending nothing happened and getting back in line. No one said a word about any of it after the initial gasps.

"I really hope I didn't ruin the ceremony..." she says, embarrassed.

"I'm pretty sure she did that herself," Ben reassures her, joining in on our conversation.

We all make our way to our tables to eat. There are a lot more people here than I expected. I know Everly didn't want a huge wedding, but there are so many people who love them both and wanted to be part of their day. Everly made sure that we all could sit next to our significant others. Though Ashley, Ben, and Jake didn't bring a plus one. I'm sitting next to Amelia, and Paige is sitting next to Matteo.

I'm surprised Paige's boyfriend came. I know they have a complicated relationship, which is understandable. James isn't a huge fan of him for good reasons. He's part of the Italian mafia. Not just part of it, his brother runs it. Regardless, Matteo is welcome because he's with Paige. Not to mention he helped save Everly when she was kidnapped. Needless to say, our security teams are extra cautious today.

Amelia and I have danced most of the reception. Either with each other, or with our friends. With the wedding winding down, I decide it's my turn to steal a dance with the bride.

"Mind if I cut in?" I ask James.

He nods and passes Everly to me.

We dance for a moment before I say, "You look gorgeous, Everly."

She smiles. "Thank you. You don't look too bad yourself."

I laugh. "Just not so bad? What happened to the days when you used to call me hot?"

She laughs this time. "That was when I was young, dumb, and single. But don't tell James, I still think you are."

"Oh, careful now. Amelia is the jealous type." I smirk.

She shakes her head. "Thank you, Bash."

"For what?" I ask.

"Everything. You've always looked out for me and acted like my older brother. I couldn't do life without you," she says sincerely.

I feel the knot in my throat tighten. I am not going to get emotional again today.

I pull her in for a hug. "I love you Everly. I hope you and James are truly happy. You deserve it."

She pulls back from the hug with tears in her eyes. "I love you too. You deserve it too, and I think Amelia is perfect for you."

Smiling, I say, "Me too."

We wrap up our sappy dance, and I head back to Amelia. On my way over, I notice Jake sneaking out of the reception hall with a bag over his shoulder. That's odd. I wonder where he's going. I shake it off, thinking I'll call him later. The reception is almost over, and I'm not going to force him to stay if he needs to go.

"Hey handsome," Amelia says, wrapping her arms around my waist.

"Hey gorgeous."

"What are your plans for tonight?" she asks innocently.

I pretend to think for a moment. "Hmm... I noticed this pretty girl staring at me all night. I was thinking about asking her to come home with me."

"Oh yeah? Who?"

I kiss her on the forehead. "You."

She laughs. "Oh good. I got worried there for a second."

I take this opportunity to finally ask her something that's been on my mind for a while now. I'm really hoping she's in the same place I am and will say yes.

"I want to ask you something," I say, pulling away from her.

"What is it?"

I pull a wrapped box out of my pocket. She stares at it and pauses for a moment before taking it out of my hand.

"I know we haven't known each other that long yet, but I know you're it for me, Amelia. I want to do life with you, and I want to come home to you every day after work. I want to be there with you on our good and bads days. I just want you with me always, baby," I say, gesturing for her to open the box.

She opens it to reveal a key card to my apartment. "Will you move in with me?"

She laughs. "You're asking me to move in with you?"

"That's what I just asked," I say nervously.

She laughs harder. "Geez Bash. I mean, I figured this box was a little too big to be a ring box, but I thought you were proposing to me."

"What if I was?" I ask seriously.

"Honestly? I would've said yes," she says.

"Really?" I let out a relieved sigh.

"Yeah, I think I would have."

"So, what about my question?" I ask.

"About moving in?" she asks innocently.

"Yes, Amelia. About moving in. Please put me out of my misery."

"Bash! I just said I would've said yes to marrying you. Why would you think I'd say no to moving in?! I'm all in Bash. I'm all in for everything with you."

I don't waste another second and kiss her hard. "I love you."

She pulls back. "I love you, too."

"I will propose to you one day, Amelia. But I've heard doing that at a wedding is rude," I say with a smirk on my face.

"Yeah, I've heard that too."

Shouts and hollers pull us back into reality. Everyone is lining up to send off the newlyweds. We get in line and throw rice as they walk by us. We watch as they get into a limo and drive off. I'm so happy for them.

"Ready?" I ask Amelia.

"Ready," she replies.

We get in the back of our car with Wells as the driver. She leans her head on me and sighs.

"Where to?" Wells asks.

"Home," I say, meeting Wells' eyes in the mirror.

He smiles, knowing that I was going to ask Amelia to move in with me today. Home. Amelia said yes, and we're going home. Our home.

Also By

Want more Bash and Amelia? Check out this bonus chapter to see a little into their future.

https://bookhip.com/KDKRTQZ

If you haven't already, read the first three books in the series! Get a glimpse of Bash in college and follow Everly and James' story in fALLINg into Summer, fALLINg into Senior Year, and fALLINg into you Again.

If you'd like the inside scoop of upcoming books and releases, join my Facebook group:

www.facebook.com/groups/snchristensenreaders

Follow me on TikTok
@authorsnchristensen

ACKNOWLEDGMENTS

There are so many who I want to thank for the success of writing and getting my books out into the world. First, and foremost, to my Lord and Savior Jesus Christ who died for my sins so I may have eternal life.

To my biggest supporter since I was little, Aunt Karen. Not only have you always been supportive of my writing and every dream I've had, but you also spent countless hours editing my books and listening to my story ideas. These books would hardly be readable without you.

To my husband, who read my stories as I wrote them, listened to every crazy idea that I had, and bounced back ideas. For taking care of the kids and allowing me to dedicate time to writing. For being understanding and taking on whatever role was needed when I was exhausted and stressed.

To Kim, for being my first official beta reader and going through each book with a fine-tooth comb to make sure the timeline is just right. For loving my characters and continuing to encourage me to write more even when I want to give up.

To Kelli, who was my first reader of my books and for being invested in the story and my characters. For understanding me and my anxiety by being there for me and texting as many times as I needed to support me.

To all my friends including Ashley, Wes, Sydney, Wendi, Jordin, and Kelly for believing in me and being excited for me to write these books. For continuing to support me through my writing journey and allowing me to share my excitement with you.

To my children, who have been patient with me and never once making me feel bad for spending time writing instead of time with you. To Amara, who constantly asked me how my book was coming along and being proud of me for being a writer. To Aiden, who graciously allowed me to go write and made me smile every time I finished for the day by being excited to see me again.

To my mother and father, who both believed in me from day one when I said I wanted to write a book. For always encouraging me to write the moment I said I wanted to be an author when I was little. For being excited and proud of me for my accomplishments.

To my ARC readers, for taking the time to read, review, and be honest about my book before it was released. For all the kind words and excitement for upcoming books and loving my characters the way I do.

And finally, to all my readers. I wrote these books because it was something that I'm passionate about. When I put them out there, I never expected anyone to actually read them. So, thank you for taking the time to read my stories and for getting invested in my characters. I can't wait to continue the stories of the characters and see where they take us.

S. N. Christensen

ABOUT THE AUTHOR

S. N. Christensen lives in a town outside of Atlanta, Georgia. She holds a BA in English and MA in Secondary Education. From a young age, she has dreamed of being a writer. She loves writing in the fantasy, thriller, and romance genres.

When she is not writing or reading, she can be found teaching at her church preschool and serving at her church. When she is at home, she loves to spend time with her husband and two children playing games and crafting.

www.ingramcontent.com/pod-product-compliance
Lightning Source LLC
Chambersburg PA
CBHW061218310726
48971CB00007B/1857